JAMIE

L. D. LAPINSKI

Orion

ORION CHILDREN'S BOOKS

First published in Great Britain in 2023 by Hodder & Stoughton

10 9 8 7 6 5 4 3

A CIP catalogue record for this book
is available from the British Library.

ISBN 978 1 510 11092 2

Typeset in Baskerville by Avon DataSet Ltd,
Alcester, Warwickshire

Printed and bound in Great Britain by Clays Ltd, Elcograf S.p.A.

The paper and board used in this book are made
from wood from responsible sources.

MIX
Paper from
responsible sources
FSC® C104740

Orion Children's Books
An imprint of Hachette Children's Group
Part of Hodder & Stoughton Limited
Carmelite House
50 Victoria Embankment
London EC4Y 0DZ

An Hachette UK Company
www.hachette.co.uk
www.hachettechildrens.co.uk

This book is for you

Have you ever had a secret?

Not a small secret, like you broke your brother's X-wing toy, or spilled your mum's nail varnish on the bed. I mean, a big secret. One that seems to get more massive every day you carry it around. The sort of secret you lie awake at night thinking about, and it starts popping into your head when you're doing ordinary stuff at school.

Have you ever had a secret like that?

My secret was a weird one. In some ways, it felt like

I'd been carrying it round my whole life, but other times it felt like it was still pretty new. It changed and squished itself around my brain all the time, invading my thoughts when I was trying to watch something or just walk home from my friends' houses. But it didn't seem to be hurting anyone, my secret. So I just carried it around with me.

It was always there though.

It whispered at me when I got dressed and when I tried to do something with my hair. It muttered louder when we went swimming with school, or when I needed to use a public toilet. It got extremely irritating when I had to go clothes shopping with Mum, though for a long time I thought that was just because I hated shopping in general. Mum used to moan as she dragged me through the racks that I wasn't being helpful, and would I just *choose* something already? And I'd point to something and she'd roll her eyes to the security cameras like she was the star of her own show and say *not* that, *I didn't mean something like* that, and the whole thing would start again.

My secret rode home with me on the bus, prodded me when a stranger talked about me. It was always there.

It got to be a sort of friend, my secret. I suppose it was better than it being my enemy. And thinking about the secret actually didn't make me feel bad. When I thought about the secret, I felt OK. Happy, even. Sometimes I felt like it was me and the secret against the world. Like only we knew the truth.

It was Year Four that I first said my secret aloud. To Ash, obviously, because you can tell anything to Ash and he won't bat an eyelid. Some people think this means he's unresponsive, but it's because he's actually really cool, and perfect at calculating risks. That time one of the kids in 5A brought a tarantula into school he just shrugged because, like he said later, it wasn't as though the spider was going to leg it across the school like an Olympic sprinter and climb up his leg. Compared to a tarantula in the backpack, what I had to say didn't seem like that much of a big deal. But even so, my legs had turned into jelly and it felt like my stomach had fallen out of my bum because what if this was the end of my friendship with Ash?

I said it quietly, so if he did shout WHAT I could pretend he'd misheard me.

'I'm not a girl or a boy, Ash.'

There was a weird sort of silence that made my lungs freeze, like the time my brother pushed me into the icy plunge-pool on holiday.

Ash blinked. 'Oh, right,' he said, looking at me with flared nostrils. Ash doesn't get wide-eyed, he gets wide-nostrilled, which is fine in summer but no good at all when winter comes and he has a perpetual cold, let me tell you. 'So. Are you still going to be called Jamie?'

'Yes,' I said, deciding right that second that Jamie was my name and I was going to stick with it. 'But don't use "he" or "she" when you're talking about me. Neither of them sound right. They're not . . . my words. You can say, "I know Jamie Rambeau, they're a super-cool person".'

Ash nodded. 'OK. I can manage that, I think. What if I forget?'

'Then I'll be really cheesed off,' I said. 'But you'll try harder not to forget next time, won't you?'

We looked at each other and smiled. I suddenly felt lighter than I had done for ages, like I'd inhaled a hundred helium balloons and I could go floating right up to the ceiling, maybe right up to the clouds or into space.

I told Daisy next. Daisy is my other best friend, and she's the one who makes the decisions and keeps me and Ash entertained at the weekends. She had more questions but got used to it, eventually.

Mum and Dad were next, and my big brother, Olly. Maybe it was a bit weird for me to tell my friends before my family, but on some level I think it annoyed me that I had to tell them at all. They were my family, they should just *know*, surely? Turns out, parents need stuff spelling out for them a lot of the time, and they're not nearly as smart as they think they are.

They had lots of questions, way more than Daisy. They wanted to know what, if anything, was going to change with my name, my clothes, my pronouns, and they even asked about my favourite video games, for some reason. But then Dad did some research and after a while they both stopped bringing it up at dinnertimes. Sometimes I wonder if they're actually OK with it or if they got bored of talking about it. And Olly? Well, he shouted HOORAY and immediately started trying to open a bottle of Mum's champagne (She stopped him before he got very far.) He came out as gay a few years

6

ago, so was delighted to have someone else in the family under the rainbow flag.

Pretty soon everyone else in my class heard about me not being a boy or a girl, and they all started using *they* when they talked about me (without me even asking!) which felt amazing. Jamie Rambeau coming out wasn't even the most interesting thing to happen that week – not when a mix-up in the school kitchens meant the creation of Double Chips Friday to get rid of a potato surplus.

But then the teachers heard about me. Things got a bit messy after that. There was a week where Mum and Dad were asked to go into school for important meetings and I had to sit there whilst they talked about me like I wasn't there and decided things without asking me. But it worked out, in the end. Mum and Dad are used to it now, and they get my words right almost all of the time, and the teachers know who I am and things are pretty good.

At least, things *were* pretty good.

Until recently.

Until we started Year Six. That was when everything went wrong.

1

'We've only just started this year and they already want us to think about a new school,' I sighed, kicking the heel of my shoe against the wall. It was late September, the summer lingering like a houseguest that's got nowhere better to be, and we were outside in the playground making the most of the late sunshine. The bell had rung two hours ago, but this evening was the annual Year Six meeting about Secondary School. The teachers had invited all of us Year Sixes to stay on the premises, to save us going home and then traipsing back again.

Me and my friends had gone outside to get some fresh air, and I'd secured an excellent seat on top of the low wall that circled the playground, with a view of the sun setting down behind the school.

'It's like they can't wait to get rid of us.'

'Can't wait to get rid of *you*,' Daisy said, grinning at me. 'Some of us they'll be devastated to see go.'

Ash spluttered. 'Daisy, last year Mr Hill said you were driving him to retirement.'

'That's only because I'm so clever I forced him to confront the truth – that he's a dried-up cornflake of a man who should have retired during the war.'

Daisy and Ash and me are all best friends. We're like one person who's been split into three, or an equilateral triangle where each of us is one of the sides and together we form a perfect shape. My mum actually calls us the Bermuda Triangle when she's ticked off with us, but we don't care. We've been best friends since we were babies, and we know everything there is to know about each other. For example, I know that Ash lets his older sister practise pedicures on him for her college course, and I know Daisy is in love with Meathead Michael Holloway from down her street, even though she pretends not to be. And they both know about the time me and Olly locked ourselves into the bathroom at our grandparents' by accident and Grandad had to climb up a ladder and through the tiny window to rescue us.

Daisy stuck a hand into her bag and rummaged around in it, in search of one of the mini Mars Bars she scattered into her bag once a week. They'd end up hidden under books and pencil cases like buried treasure and sometimes they'd get super-squashed and end up looking like caramel slugs, but she'd still eat them. 'The teachers would have us all working down a mine if they could, anyway. You heard Mr Hill when we went to look around the gallery in town – he said we should all be "out earning a crust instead of learning about drama and art".'

I snorted. Mr Hill and I hadn't exactly been best buddies. By the end of the last year, he had refused to talk to me or about me at all. That was great in some ways because it meant I never got picked on to answer questions about algebra, but it was pants in other ways because Mr Hill was in charge of the school football team, and if he didn't like you, you didn't get in.

Luckily, Miss Palanska, our Year Six teacher, is the exact opposite of him. She runs the drama club and wears pencils stuffed into her pink hair and has lots of tattoos. She had offered to throw our class a pizza party since we'd all had to stay late at school for this meeting. When most teachers say 'pizza party' they mean a damp finger of supermarket pizza warmed over a candle, but Palanska had got the good stuff delivered, and had even remembered to order some vegan options. The way to her students' hearts was paved with pizza-shaped bribes and we absolutely loved her for it. It had been a great afternoon.

'Any thoughts about schools?' Miss Palanska had asked, sitting on her desk. She'd put some old Tom and Jerry cartoons on the whiteboard and they were half-projected onto her arm so Jerry kept running through her and disappearing. 'Don't be shy if you want to ask questions, it can be a bit worrying going to a big new place, I know.'

'How come St Joseph's has got a swimming pool?' Grace Pavers asked in annoyance. She was one of those sporty kids who you just know is going to be on TV one day winning a million gold medals. 'And Queen Elizabeth's has only got a football pitch?'

Palanska grinned. 'I'm not sure I can help with the lack of swimming pool, Grace. I was thinking more . . . is anyone worried about the actual learning experience?'

'I am.' Weedy Pavel Gabrielczyk put his hand up.

'I don't even know what an essay is, and they say we're going to have to write loads of them.'

'An essay is like a book report,' Palanska said kindly. 'And they'll show you how to write one, they're not going to sit you down for an exam as soon as you get through the door.' She got up and dusted off her hands. Then she came over to my table where I was playing HangNoughts with Daisy and Ash. HangNoughts is a game we invented in the summer – it's a cross between Hangman and Noughts and Crosses. Ash had a whole notebook full of the rules, though we'd never actually had chance to teach anyone else.

We looked up as Miss Palanska came over. She stared down at the game, which we play on squared paper that Daisy pinches from the Maths cupboard. 'You three alright?' she asked quietly.

Ash doesn't like being talked to by teachers, even nice ones, and he constantly worries that we're going to get done for using the maths paper without asking, so he just went red and looked away, leaving Daisy and me to smile.

'We're good,' I said. 'Thanks for the pizza party.'

'Oh, you're welcome, sweetheart. Are *you* OK with schools, and everything?' she asked me.

'Big school doesn't scare me,' I said. 'It's just going to be the same as this.'

'Except bigger,' Daisy said, drawing a line through three noughts. 'Hangman.'

'What?' Ash blurted out, leaning over to see.

Miss Palanska's eyes moved from me to Daisy and then to Ash and back to me, and I noticed a tiny frown crease itself between her eyebrows. 'But I did wonder, Jamie . . .' she started to say.

'MISS! MISS!! PAVEL'S GOT HIS ELBOW IN THE GARLIC DIP!' Grace suddenly screeched from across the room.

Palanska turned away to deal with Pavel, and whatever she had been going to say had to be put on hold. I didn't think any more about it. It's amazing how much I wasn't thinking about, right then.

But honestly, it's a wonder kids aren't constantly levitating with worry, especially Year Sixes. We're given heaps of worries from September onwards, and it's pretty much impossible to handle them all. You've got to pick a few to focus on and let the others sort of wash over you or you'll lose your mind. I was worried about SATs, and my grandma's dog Jellybean because she was old, and about Olly, who had decided only the weekend before last to become a goth (and then got grounded the next day for getting black lipstick all over the new white towels). I wasn't really worried about myself because I was happy with myself.

But I was about to find out that, despite what I'd thought, not everyone else was happy with me. The meeting that evening turned out to be just the start.

Right then though, I was too busy laughing at Ash trying to wangle a non-squished mini-Mars from Daisy. She was offering him a squashed one, trying to convince him they were just as good.

'There's Mum,' she suddenly said, grinning as she was given an excuse to get away from Ash's pestering. She put a flat chocolate into Ash's hand, then hopped down from the wall and skipped over to her mum, waving. Me and Ash got down more reluctantly and walked over like we were in slow motion. Daisy's mum, Denise, isn't a horrible person, exactly, she's just one of those parents who you're never quite sure about. She does a lot of what Ash calls Extreme Eye Contact (or EEC), which neither of us like because it's like she's trying to see right into our minds. She did EEC a *lot* to me when I first told her about myself. She used to cuddle me and call me Jamie Jamster when we were little but after I told everyone I was non-binary she started treating me like a little green alien from Jupiter, speaking extra-loud and slow in case I'd forgotten how to understand English.

'Why has she come dressed as the Cookie Monster?' Ash whispered under his breath, and I had to try hard not to explode because it was true – Denise was wearing a fluffy blue coat which made her look like she lived on Sesame Street.

I've always suspected that Denise isn't a fan of Ash, either – that she mistakes him being quiet for being rude. It isn't Ash's fault he's so reserved, not everyone is an open book. And if you take the time to really get to know him, you find out he's the nicest person ever, and he is so caring about the people he likes. But Daisy's mum hasn't got the patience to try. I dread to think what she says about us to Daisy when we're not there.

'Hel-LO, Jamie,' she said when we got close enough, stretching out the words like toffee. She gave me one of those fake smiles that don't reach the eyes, and screwed up her nose like a hamster. 'And Ash. Gosh, haven't you grown!'

'Hi, Mrs Adewumi,' Ash said to the ground.

'Hi, Denise,' I said in a normal voice. 'I like your coat.' Ash gave me a horrified look, but Denise beamed at me.

'Thank you, sweetheart, got it in Matalan. Reduced to a tenner, can you believe it?' She preened, and I gave her a smile whilst Ash kept looking at the ground to hide the fact that his face was twitching the way it does when he's trying not to laugh. 'Are your parents here yet, Jamie?' she asked, suddenly turning on the EEC so strong that I was sure she could describe the inside of my skull with perfect accuracy.

'They got here ten minutes ago.' I pointed at the reception. 'You know them, they had to go get front row seats.'

Denise nodded, somehow still managing not to blink. 'Oh, I don't blame them for that. Difficult enough as it is trying to see who's on that little stage, sometimes you can hardly hear what they're saying, either. Speaking of which, we'd better get inside, don't you think? Come on, Daisy.' She gave me another one of those wide fake smiles, and clamped her hands down on Daisy's shoulders to steer her towards the school.

Ash and I gave them a bit of a head start before following. 'Why does she talk to you like you're simple?' Ash asked, asking the obvious like he always did.

'Because she thinks I am. She thinks Daisy's an undiscovered genius and that you and me are holding her back and being bad influences in every way possible.'

'Are we?' Ash asked in alarm.

'Of course not. We're amazing influences. Especially you.' I patted him on the shoulder. 'But you know what Denise is like. She wants Daisy to be what she thinks is normal, not what's actually normal. She probably wishes she could get Daisy away from us both.'

Ash pushed his glasses up his nose. 'Well, she's not going to have much luck, unless she locks her away and home-schools her or something.'

'No chance, Daisy's still traumatised after home-schooling during lockdown. She'd run away from home, I think. Anyway, she loves school. She's already bought her uniform for Queen Elizabeth's.'

Ash kicked at the concrete underfoot. 'I don't want to be at school without Daisy next year,' he said. 'I don't know how to do stuff when she isn't around. She tells me what to do.'

'Because she's a bossy-boots.'

'No. I mean, yeah she is, sometimes. But I meant because she's just good at getting things started. Games, or projects, or going places. She's good at that.'

'She is,' I agreed. 'Don't worry, you'll see each

other after school every day I bet, and weekends and holidays. It's going to be fine. Promise.' There wasn't anything else I could do or say. We'd always been together, the three of us, ever since we were in Nursery. It started when Denise and Sana – that's Ash's mum – had invited my mum out for a coffee after playgroup. At the beginning, because we were babies and couldn't even roll away from each other, we pretty much *had* to be friends. But soon we realised we liked each other for real. Over ten years, we had become the perfect team. It sucked that this was the last year we were going to be at school together. A decade of friendship, about to be brought to a sudden end by the joint efforts of Queen Elizabeth's and St Joseph's Secondary Schools.

I spotted my parents as soon as we went into the hall – they were at the front, just as I had predicted, leaflets in their hands and looking keenly at the empty stage like they were frightened of missing something. Dad had come wearing an actual suit, and Mum was in a dress. No one else's parents were dressed like they were here for a business meeting, not even Pavel's mum, who owns three of the shops in town (she was wearing a metallic purple tracksuit and her plastic nails were clacking on her phone as she emailed frantically). My parents had left a seat between them for me so I would be unable to talk to anyone or escape.

'You nearly missed the start,' Mum hissed as I sat down. 'Where've you been?'

'I've been playing in the middle of the road with scissors and broken glass,' I said, which was my usual answer when Mum asked where I'd been.

'Don't be cheeky, the teachers will hear you. You're supposed to be making a good impression.'

'Unless they're invisible, I don't think anyone is there yet,' I said, gesturing at the empty stage.

Mum gave me a look. 'Very funny. So where were you really?'

'I was just outside with Daisy and Ash,' I said with a sigh.

Mum's lips went thin. She never criticised my friends out loud, she just pulled faces instead. It was rich, when their parents were *her* friends. *I don't understand why Daisy/Ash* can't be more like his/her* mum/dad** she would complain after every time they came round.

Dad handed me the two leaflets he'd been holding. 'Read these while you're waiting.'

I dutifully opened the first leaflet.

And it was like being punched in the face.

Maybe it sounds stupid, but I'd never actually given any thought to where I was going after Year Six was over. I was just going to secondary school and that was that.

---

* delete as applicable

We'd spent the last few years being beaten with an imaginary stick about SATs and results and achievement, and what came after that felt too big and too bright to look at, like the sun. I knew secondary school was coming, and I knew there was a choice of schools, but until I opened the leaflet for Queen Elizabeth's High School for Girls, I hadn't realised I would need to make that choice. Because in our town, there were two small secondary schools. One for boys – which was St Joseph's Academy – and the other for girls.

There wasn't another option. You went to one, or you went to the other. The closest school after those was in the city, over an hour away on the bus. I hadn't let myself worry about the school options, until that exact moment as I sat in the hall, holding the leaflets and feeling my hands go as cold as when you're hunting for choc ices in the freezer.

'Mum?' I asked in a small voice. 'Mum, I—'

'Shh.' She flapped her hand at me. 'It's starting.'

And it was. Two teachers had swept onto the stage and were waiting for quiet, which came quickly. They beamed in that *I'm so happy to see you*! way that teachers do at the start of the year before they start dishing out detentions, and each of them stood beside a projector screen that had been wheeled onto the stage. The screens showed the logos for each school: a cross on a blue shield for St Joseph's, and a crown above a tree for Queen Elizabeth's.

'Good evening, parents,' the first teacher, a man, called.

The woman gave a little giggle. 'And good evening, boys and girls.'

'And everyone else,' I added, in a whisper that made Mum nudge me. I scowled. Our teachers didn't say 'boys and girls' anymore. They said 'everyone'. That was because last year I had mentioned it to Ash's mum, who is a parent governor, and when she heard about how it made me feel she took it upon herself to get the head teacher, Ms Lovell, to change it. It didn't take any effort to include everyone in your greeting.

'Welcome to our little presentation,' the man said. 'I'm Mr Dean, I'm the headmaster——'

'Head teacher,' I muttered.

'——of St Joseph's, and this is Mrs Bailey, headmistress——'

'Teacher,' I repeated, this time getting a glare from my dad for my trouble.

'——of Queen Elizabeth's. We know next year seems long way off right now, but we thought if we showed everyone what to expect, then you can feel prepared. We're going to start off with a video, it'll be played on both screens, so hopefully everyone can see . . .' Mr Dean pressed a button on the remote and a video started to play.

I can't tell you what was in the rest of the presentation exactly, because as soon as the video started playing I went into a sort of trance. I remember that there were lots of images of things like the boys' uniform and the girls' uniform, and the boys' swimming pool and the girls' football pitch, and the boys' theatre classes and the girls' gardening, and each school's trips and camps and exams and . . .

Everything was so separate. For the first time, I felt properly on my own. Everyone at my primary school wore the same uniform and PE kit, we all used the same toilets and cloakroom and we were together for everything. There hadn't been any separate rules for boys and girls until now, because we were just kids, treated the same.

But now everything was separate and it felt wrong.

Then it was over, and our head teacher Ms Lovell was on the stage thanking the two other Heads for coming and saying wasn't that worthwhile watching, everyone?

And then she announced that coffees and teas would be served now and everyone was welcome to mingle.

'That was lovely, wasn't it?' Mum smiled down at me. 'Jamie?'

I couldn't even move my head. I felt frozen to my chair, turned to a statue, left behind on a shelf like something broken or not wanted. All around me, people were laughing and chatting and talking happily about the school trips and lessons. I had been left behind.

All the time the presentation had been going on, I had been waiting for someone to speak up. I wanted someone who *wasn't* me to realise that they had talked about boys and girls but not non-binary kids like me. That they'd focussed on girls and boys but never once mentioned non-binary kids like me. I really, really wanted someone, anyone, to point it out to the people on the stage. I needed Ash or Daisy or my parents – just anyone who wasn't me – to put their hand up, to prove they had thought of non-binary people, to ask what was in place for us.

Someone had to have noticed, surely.

Someone would have seen how binary it all was, wouldn't they?

But everyone was getting up out of their seats, and politely queueing for drinks, and not a single person seemed to have realised that I'd been left out.

I was going to have to speak up for myself.

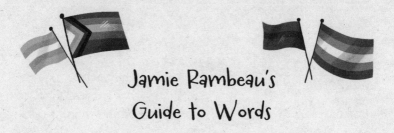

Jamie Rambeau's Guide to Words

Cisgender/Cis – When you're cool and happy being known as the gender the midwife said you were when you were born

Transgender/Trans – When you're not

Some people who are non-binary like to say they're transgender as well, some don't. Like everything, it's up to you which labels you want to wear. Personally, I feel like 'non-binary' on its own is more Me.

2

I'm not used to making a fuss. I'd suggested the *good morning, everyone* greeting and I'd asked Ms Lovell to buy some books with non-binary characters for the school library, but that was it. I hadn't had to do much else, because nothing else had felt wrong in school. And in the wider world, I didn't feel big enough to change things. This, though – this felt different. Like I might not get another chance to put it right. I had to tell them they'd forgotten about me.

As always, my parents were the first people in the

queue. They'd got their coffees and had gone over to the head teachers and were clearly just about to politely simper about how much they'd enjoyed the presentation, when I opened my big mouth.

'Excuse me. Your school's just for boys, is it?' I asked Mr Dean.

He gave me a confused blink. 'Er, yes,' he said uncertainly. He probably thought I was stupid.

'And yours is just for girls?' I asked, turning to Mrs Bailey.

'Jamie,' my mother said in a heavy warning voice. But I'd started, and if I was going to get into trouble I might as well do it properly.

'That's right, er, dear,' the teacher said to me, her eyes darting over my uniform, looking for a clue as to what I might be. Pointless, as everyone at our school wears the same trousers and a pullover.

I nodded. 'OK, so if there's a school for boys, and a

school for girls . . . then where am I supposed to go?'

The blank stares I got in reply were extremely annoying. I had to try hard not to lose my temper.

Ms Lovell must have smelled danger because she suddenly appeared out of thin air between me and my opponents. 'This is Jamie Rambeau, one of our Year Sixes,' she said smoothly. 'A future star on the stage, I think. They've got a lot of confidence for their age.'

'Your Year Sixes have?' Mr Dean frowned.

'No, *Jamie* has. They're in the drama club, which has really helped their confidence. I think they're going to do brilliantly in secondary school.' Ms Lovell was trying, without saying it directly, to tell the visitors that I was non-binary. She was dropping the fact I use *they* and *them* instead of *he* or *she*, as incredibly obvious clues for the other adults to pick up on. Unfortunately, like most grown-ups, they were rather slow on the uptake.

'Alright,' Mr Dean said with a little shrug. 'Nice

to meet you, Jamie . . .' His eyes slid past me like he was going to say hello to the next family, but I wasn't having that.

'I asked you a question,' I said, louder. 'I want to know which school I'll be going to.'

'Jamie, this isn't the place,' my mum said, now red in the face.

'But they're both here,' I pointed out. 'This is where we're meant to ask stuff, isn't it? One of them wants boys and one wants girls, but no one wants me. Or has everyone forgotten about me?'

'I don't think I understand,' Mrs Bailey said, frowning over her glasses at me.

Ms Lovell got there before I did, raising a finger like a sword ready for battle. 'I think, perhaps, we should have a *private* meeting,' she said, looking pointedly at the queue of parents. 'So we can discuss this properly.'

'I think that's a wonderful idea,' Mum said quickly.

'I'm sorry for taking up so much of your time,' she added to the teachers.

'Not at all,' Mr Dean said, still looking at me oddly.

'Come on, Jamie,' Dad said, propelling me out of the line so hurriedly he spilled lukewarm coffee down his sleeve.

*

'I do wish you wouldn't make such a *fuss*,' Mum said. 'Honestly, everyone was listening, Jamie, why couldn't you have just let it lie?'

We were driving home and she was in the fifth solid minute of telling me off. I'd made a mistake by letting her build up steam as we were leaving, and now that we were on the main road, she was an unstoppable force of ranting nature.

'I couldn't *just let it lie*, because I don't know what school I'm going to,' I said when she paused to inhale. 'And who cares if everyone was listening? It's not like I said anything that's a secret, is it? I'm not some gremlin you have to hide away.'

'But not everyone understands,' Mum said. 'Not everyone gets this . . . non-binary thing.'

Anger suddenly burned in my chest. 'I'm not a thing.'

'I never said you were, stop being ridiculous and twisting what I say. Not everyone understands though. They can get the wrong idea.'

Dad said nothing; he was concentrating extremely hard on the road.

'And anyway,' Mum carried on, 'which school did you think you'd be going to?'

'I hadn't thought about it,' I said honestly, but guiltily, like I'd made a mistake. 'But it's not my problem to sort out. They should take non-binary kids into consideration when they're setting up their schools. It's unfair.'

'Unfair!' Mum scoffed.

'Well, it is,' I said, my voice shrinking as hers grew.

'They didn't think about me.'

'Those schools were around before you. Before even me or your dad were born!' Mum said, starting to get rather shrill. 'They've existed for longer than . . . your new ideas.'

I stared hard at the back of her head. 'OK. What did *you* think was going to happen with schools then?'

She sighed, but didn't answer. We drove the rest of the way home in a cold silence that practically frosted over the upholstery. When we got home, Dad got out of the car without saying anything, and marched inside before I'd even got my belt off. Mum unbuckled her own seat belt and turned around to look at me.

'I don't mean to get short with you, you know that,' she said gently, though there was still a rage-muscle throbbing in her cheek. 'I know it's important to you, but the world is a lot bigger than you think, sweetheart. Not everyone understands what non-binary means, and some people might even get angry about it. Sometimes, it's just better to keep your head down and avoid confrontation.'

'But no one else has to keep their heads down,' I said. 'Why should I keep quiet about who I am? You don't see anyone else not talking about their gender. Everyone else is allowed to talk about themselves as much as they want.'

'That's because everyone else is *normal*, Jamie,' she snapped.

It felt as if she'd slapped me.

She knew she'd messed up, because she instantly reached for my hand, her eyes going shiny. 'Jamie, I'm sorry, I didn't mean—'

But I was already out of the car, through the front door and up the stairs.

*

I'd thought Mum and Dad had always been cool about people who were LGBTQ. Dad's cousin Martin is married to a man and my parents always talked about how lovely they are as a couple and how well-behaved their kids are. I remember Mum got angry at the TV once, when an author was being shouted at by a presenter about being included on a prize list for books written by women. The presenter thought the author didn't count as a woman because she was trans. Mum wrote and complained to the TV company and she bought five copies of the book to give out to her friends.

So I thought they were fine with me being non-binary. They hadn't shouted or screamed or threatened to disown me when I'd come out to them. They'd just sat there and listened, and asked questions. And afterwards, we never talked about it. At the time, I counted myself lucky – you've only got to be online for five minutes to see horror stories of coming-outs that went wrong, of people who'd lost their families because of who they are. I thought I was lucky.

I'm not sure about that now.

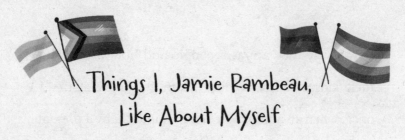

Things I, Jamie Rambeau, Like About Myself

1. My hair is a fantastic shade of brown – it looks the way brownie mixture does when you stir white chocolate into it because it's got dark and light streaks that get more pronounced in the sunshine

2. I'm super-strong. I can carry seven stacked-up chairs at once when it's our class's turn to tidy up the hall after assembly

3. I can read at the speed of light. I often read a book every day after school. I could probably read an entire library in a week or so

4. I can't roll my tongue. This is a very rare thing, because if your mum OR your dad can do it, then you can do it, too. But none of my family can

5. I'm not a girl or a boy. I am an amazing non-binary human and I am so happy about that

3

'Thank you for coming in,' Ms Lovell said, leading us into her office.

My parents were both there, along with Mrs Bailey from Queen Elizabeth's. Mr Dean had apparently decided not to come. I couldn't decide if that made me feel better or worse.

'I'm glad we can get together and have this chat,' Ms Lovell said as she sat down in her Official Head Teacher Chair behind the desk.

I was in a grotty mood from what Mum had said the

night before, but I tried to keep my expression polite. Ms Lovell had never given me a hard time, exactly. But she did look as though she was wishing that I didn't exist right now. She probably would have preferred the biggest thorn in her side to be school inspectors, or the fact there was asbestos in the staff room, but instead she'd been landed with me.

Mrs Bailey from Queen Elizabeth's, on the other hand, was giving me a huge beaming smile that reminded me of a wide-mouthed tree-frog. I found myself hoping she wasn't about to unhinge her jaw and swallow me whole.

'Now, this is a bit of a pickle,' Ms Lovell said, folding her hands together. 'We need to be careful and considered about this whole thing, because we've never had a, er, situation like this before. Always boys and girls. Never someone who's a bit of both.'

'I'm not a bit of both,' I said, more snappishly than

I meant to. 'I'm neither.'

All the adults in the room did long, slow blinks as if in a group prayer to the god of patience.

'Thank you,' Ms Lovell said, after a moment. 'That's just the sort of thing I mean. You're the expert here, Jamie, and as much as I don't want to put you on the spot, you will need to tell us off if we mess up. Some of us are quite old and not all up to date with these new ideas, I'm afraid.'

You're supposed to say sorry, *not* thank you *if you mess up*, I thought, but didn't say anything. I gave a bit of a tree-frog smile myself and the adults relaxed a bit. I wanted to tell Ms Lovell that being non-binary wasn't a new idea at all, that people like me have always been around, everywhere in the world, it's just that it's new to *her*.

'It's not really a new idea,' I said, trying to sound polite. 'There's lots of non-binary cultures and people out there. Nepal actually has a third gender category on official documents.' There was more I wanted to say, but I wanted to seem co-operative so I decided to let someone else have a go at speaking.

'I thought you were very brave, Jamie, coming and asking your questions outright yesterday,' Mrs Bailey said brightly. 'It's not something I've ever had to consider before. Now, at Queen Elizabeth's we pride ourselves greatly on our inclusion, and we have had several transgender girls come to the school—'

'I'm not a girl though,' I said. 'I'm not a trans girl or a cis girl.'

Mrs Bailey swatted at me, which is what adults do when they interrupt. 'I didn't mean to say you were, I simply meant that we are . . . used to children who have gender issues.'

I forced myself to ignore that last bit. My gender was only an issue for people who wanted it to be. 'But you still only take girls, in your school for girls.'

'It is a girls' school, yes. But I'm hoping we can all make this work, if we pull together.' Mrs Bailey smiled and I realised she was dangling the opportunity to go to her school in front of me like a worm on a hook. It felt just as appetising.

I folded my arms. Daisy would be going to that school. She already had the uniform, with the blazer and tie and skirt and knee-socks. She was looking forward to the residential trips, and the netball team, and the award-winning school library. And as much as I would have loved to be with Daisy, and devour every book in the library and blow things up in the science labs . . . it was a *girls'* school. It wasn't a school for me.

And what about Ash? He was really bad at making new friends, he'd never survive on his own . . . He needed me with him at St Joseph's, didn't he? But that was a school for boys and that wasn't for me either. My heart suddenly sank right down into my shoes, and I sagged in my chair. Whatever happened, I was going to end up leaving one of my best friends behind.

When it was clear I wasn't going to say anything affirmative to Mrs Bailey, my dad leaned forward and cleared his throat. 'There must be some precedent we can look at – some other child in Jamie's situation.'

'It's difficult to find out that sort of thing,' Ms Lovell said, with the air of someone who'd spent a lot of time on Google recently. She even jerked her head towards her computer on her desk. 'Because of privacy laws, you understand. There could well be other non-binary children who have been faced with this decision, but we wouldn't know about it.'

My mum gave her temples a massage. Normally after school she does yoga and drinks a green tea whilst I do my homework, and I could tell she was desperate to leave. 'We don't want Jamie to be a sort of . . .

experiment,' she said. 'Surely the local authority could tell us *something.*'

'I'm afraid not, Mrs Rambeau.'

'Forgive me for being frank,' Mrs Bailey interrupted again, 'but as far as I understand, you can't legally change your gender until you're eighteen, is that correct?'

This made me want to sink right through the chair and disappear completely. Technically, Mrs Bailey was correct, but it wasn't even as simple as changing your gender marker the day you turn eighteen. There's a whole process, and you need to get a Gender Recognition Certificate. And to get one of those, you have to have seen a doctor and been diagnosed with something called *gender dysphoria*. My GP referred me to the gender clinic when I was ten, but the waiting list to be seen at the clinic is currently FOUR YEARS LONG. So, I'll be fourteen by the time I get my first appointment, and then I'll have to have even more appointments before they'll say I've got *gender dysphoria*. BUT GUESS WHAT. Even if I do all that *and* wait till I'm eighteen, I still won't be able to legally change my gender to non-binary. That's not allowed in the UK yet.

Legally, I don't exist.

It's a bit like being a spy, only without the cool gadgets and the fancy car. Maybe things will change in the future, and they'll take the M or F off things like passports and driving licences altogether. But right now, if you're non-binary, you have to choose.

Mrs Bailey was still speaking. '. . . and, taking that into account, since Jamie can't legally change his or her gender yet, can I ask what they're down as on the school register? M or F?'

I made a choking noise as my brain short-circuited. 'You can't ask that!' I blurted out.

'It might be helpful when it comes to admissions,' Mrs Bailey went on. 'You can keep calling yourself . . .

this or that . . . whatever you like! But the legal marker is what—'

'You're not allowed to ask that,' I repeated, hoping it was true. 'You can't ask me what someone thought I was when I was born. It doesn't mean anything, anyway.'

'That *is* an inappropriate question.' Ms Lovell thankfully came to back me up. 'We really can't divulge confidential—'

'Well Jamie was obviously born as *something*,' Mrs Bailey said, her face suddenly going blotchy the way faces do when their owners have been caught out doing something wrong and they're just going to keep talking in the hopes the embarrassment will go away (it never does).

'It's none of your business!' I squeaked, but no one was listening to me anymore.

Mrs Bailey was steaming ahead like an engine. 'Look, I can't offer you more than what I offer any pupil, Jamie. A school, for girls. That's all it will ever be. I know

Mr Dean would say the same about St Joseph's for boys. We are happy to have you, but we will be accepting you as a girl, whatever letter you've got on the register. We can't accept you as some third, made-up option. You can't roll out your imaginary gender and expect the world to lean over backwards for you and change—'

After that it gets a bit fuzzy, because my vision went red and I told Mrs Bailey to do something that was extremely rude. I ended up sitting in the corridor whilst Mum and Dad said sorry over and over for my behaviour and not one person apologised to me.

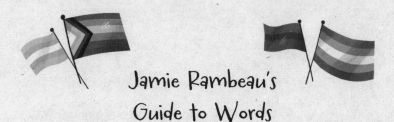

Jamie Rambeau's Guide to Words

Discrimination

Discrimination means someone treating you unfairly because of who you are.

It is against the law to discriminate against anyone because of their:

- age

- gender

- disability

- race

- religion or belief, or

- sexual orientation

. . . but that doesn't seem to stop a lot of people.

4

Once you realise how binary the world is, it's difficult to see things any other way. *Binary* means that there's two options, one or the other, and your choice has to be one of the two. Like computer code being all ones and zeros. Like left or right, up or down. Like M or F.

The world can be so hecking binary when it comes to gender, it's actually hilarious.

Walk into a clothes shop. You've got Women's on one side, and Men's on the other. Women's and Men's toilets (except in your own home where apparently it's fine to have a free-for-all). Women's soaps and smells and stuff, and Men's. Even things like books are split up, which is bonkers. Once you see it, you can't unsee it. Then you start to wonder where the stuff is for non-binary people. Well, the truth is that anyone should be able to wear anything, read anything or smell like anything they want to. There's actually no rules about it, at least not here in the UK. No one will stop you if you're a girl and you want to buy Crushed Soldering Iron-scented soap. So you have to wonder . . .

. . . why do they split everything up in the first place?

Ash says it's about money. He says companies can sell more stuff because this way families have to buy one soap for the boys in the house and one for the girls, instead of just one soap for everyone. Daisy says it's because parents want to show everyone what kind of baby they have. Pink for a girl, blue for a boy. Can't have anyone wondering what sort of baby you've got, can you?

But why is it so important that people know? Why is it so important that men don't buy Floral Spring body wash or wear skirts? Why can't I decide I want to buy a dress *and* a pack of boxer shorts?

Why aren't the clothes grouped by type? A trousers section and a skirts section and a jumpers section?

These sorts of questions are why Mum doesn't bring me shopping anymore.

*

I expected to be grounded for what happened in Ms Lovell's office, but instead my parents opted for the punishment where we don't speak about what happened and they just leave me to stew in my own juice. Which is worse, in some ways, because I always worry they'll change their minds and take my iPad away after all. I spent the next few days tip-toeing around them, trying not to draw attention to myself, and bolting down my dinners like they were going to be snatched away before legging it upstairs every night.

Unfortunately, there was plenty of attention at school. I don't know who spread it, but the story of me telling Mrs Bailey to go and do *that* was all round the school by the next lunchtime. Half the kids saw me as a hero and the other half as a dangerous delinquent. After a full day of everyone pretending to dive for cover whenever I stood up or spoke, I was sick of it.

'I'm guessing you didn't decide on a school, then?' Daisy asked as we piled out of school at the end of the day. I knew she'd be the one to ask. Ash had been avoiding the subject all day, paralysed with fear that my new reputation was going to rub off on him and his mum would find out. She probably already knew.

'No, I didn't choose one. I don't know what to do about it.' I hitched my Spider-Man backpack up as we walked. 'I have to go to one of the schools, that's pretty much decided. But it's like, either way I lose. I lose you, or Ash, or my identity. I don't . . .'

'Don't want things to change,' Ash finished for me, quietly.

I just looked at him, my heart suddenly as heavy as a small moon. Because it was true. I wanted things to stay as they were, forever if possible. I wanted it to be the three of us, all together, with no one caring who or what we were. Just playing and messing about and inventing games and stuff. But it didn't seem like that was going to be possible.

Daisy didn't seem sad, though. 'Can't you just go to one of the schools and still say you're non-binary?' she asked.

'That's what Mrs Bailey suggested,' I sighed. 'She said I'd have to be an F on the register if I went to Queen Elizabeth's, but I could call myself anything I wanted. Maybe that's as good as it's going to get. But . . . it'll still be pretending to be something I'm not.

I've been doing that for almost my whole life, I don't want to go back to doing it.'

'No one in your classes would see the register, though?'

'No, but *I'd* know,' I insisted. 'Plus, it's still a school for girls. So everyone would just assume I was one. I'd have to come out over and over again. I don't want to have to do that.'

Daisy and Ash didn't say anything.

I kicked the pavement. 'Neither of the schools want me there as I am, that's the long and short of it. They want me to pick M or F and pretend. I don't want to have to. No one else has to, why should I? Mrs Bailey even called being non-binary *imaginary*. That why I swore at her.'

Ash's nostrils widened. 'Oh, no.'

'Oh, yes.'

'Well, she deserved it,' Daisy said, flicking her braids over her shoulder. 'You can't change who you are, and you're not imaginary. You're you. How can you choose to be something you're not?'

'Mum and Dad wouldn't mind me choosing,' I said, darkly. I hadn't meant to talk about my parents, but now I felt like a boiling pan, starting to overflow because the heat was too high. 'It's all coming out, now. Mum thinks I'm abnormal and Dad keeps using my name to avoid saying 'they' when he talks about me. They never used to be like this, either of them. When I first told them, they were fine. I don't get why things have changed.'

Ash gave one of his deep sighs, which sound like he's pulled them from deep inside a well. '*Were* they fine?'

I blinked. 'What do you mean?'

'Well, you told me they didn't hug you or anything,' he said quietly.

I opened my mouth to say that wasn't the point, that the point was they hadn't been angry or sad, but . . .

Ash was right. They hadn't smiled or hugged me or told me they were happy about me being non-binary. They'd just nodded.

Daisy looked confused. 'I don't get it. If they've always felt like this, why didn't they say anything at the time?'

Ash chose that moment to drop one of his unusually perceptive sentences. 'They didn't think it would be forever.'

Daisy and I looked at him.

'It's the facts,' he said softly. 'They thought you'd grown out of it, like you grew out of your Pokémon obsession. They thought you'd eventually choose: boy or girl, man or woman. They didn't think you'd grow up to be a non-binary adult.'

'There are loads of non-binary adults,' I said.

'Who?' Daisy asked curiously.

I started reeling them off. 'Jonathan Van Ness, Demi Lovato, Sam Smith, Indya Moore . . . There's even

Olympic athletes like Timothy LeDuc and Alana Smith. It's not a phase, it's forever.'

'We know that,' Ash said. 'But maybe your parents didn't. Now that they're realising it's forever, they'll be wondering what's going to happen when you start growing up. You know . . .' He trailed off into a whisper. '*Puberty*.'

My already red face went redder. When I went to my doctor last year, she said I could decide what I wanted to do when I was older. Was that *now*? All the kids in my class still looked like kids, except for Big Danny Hovis who had already started shaving. But then – why did I need to do anything? I didn't need to change my body because I was non-binary.

'That doesn't necessarily matter,' I said. 'You don't need to look a certain way to be non-binary.'

'Oh, OK, that's good then,' Daisy said, accepting this. 'But . . . even so . . . you'll still have to choose a school and leave one of us behind, won't you?'

'I guess,' I said. 'But I don't know how to choose. Right now I'll settle for making it out of this term alive.'

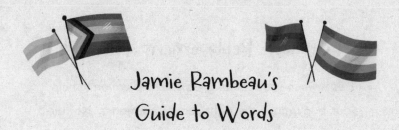

Jamie Rambeau's
Guide to Words

Hormones

Hormones are chemicals that whizz around your body telling it to do different jobs. When you get to puberty, hormones tell your body how to grow, depending on what chemicals it's got whizzing around.

Puberty Blockers

Sometimes you can start puberty early. If this is a problem, doctors can give you medicine called puberty blockers to stop the process for a bit until you're ready to start it again.

Transgender kids can also have puberty blockers to stop them going through the wrong kind of puberty for their true gender (because some of the changes that happen during puberty can't be reversed).

Hormone Replacement Therapy

This is when your doctor gives you medication to help your body make the right sort of hormones. Not all transgender people choose to have this, but the hormones can help your body develop and change like it was supposed to.

5

Secondary schools had to take a backseat in the hyper-expressway of my mind for a few weeks after that, because we started doing mock SATs, and they are The Worst. Some kids were losing sleep and crying over it. Ash started carrying a special stress ball around with him shaped like a 20-sided dice and he squeezed it so much that by the end of the week of mocks it had been squished into a sphere. Daisy started having tutoring after school in front of the laptop, but she said the man teaching her spent most of the lesson trying to take himself off mute.

I'm not clever enough to have to worry about getting top grades, but I'm not at the bottom of the class either so there's no pressure not to fail either. It's nice to be average at something. Mum says I could do better if I tried, but I don't know what she thinks I'm doing in these tests – I'm not exactly chilling out on a lilo with a Diet Coke and my sunglasses on.

By the time the tests were over, it was October.

On the first Saturday of the month, Ash came over to my house, and Mum made a giant fuss of him like she always does. She must have really been in a good mood because she let us use Dad's PlayStation 5 to play *Dracula Death Mansion* which is technically an 18, but if we keep the sound turned down she pretends not to hear the swearing and screaming.

'Are you looking forward to going to St Joseph's, Ash?' she asked later, bringing us pizza.

'I don't know. It'll be OK, I think.' Ash filled his

mouth with a pizza slice. He still gets nervous around my mum even though he's known her all his life and she used to change his nappies as a baby. Maybe that's *why* he gets nervous.

'It's got a swimming pool, hasn't it?' Mum pressed on. 'And a proper theatre stage?'

Ash doesn't care about sports or plays, so he just shrugged. But my interest was prickled, because I like theatre. I wouldn't mind being an actor, actually. I love being in the drama club at school. Last year we did Bugsy Malone and we had real splurge guns that shot out tons of shaving foam. The caretaker went bananas at the state of the carpets after the performance.

Mum was still talking. 'They have amazing school trips. I was talking to her next door, her lads have a great time there. I'm sure you'll really enjoy yourself at St Joseph's, Ash.'

I looked up, forgetting to pause my game so my

character got piled on by three vampires. 'Why've you been asking next door about St Joseph's?'

'It's good to know what people think of places,' she said, calm as you like. 'I'll be asking about Queen Elizabeth's as well, don't get yourself in a twist.'

I relaxed sightly, though I was still tense. I'd started to get a horrible sicky knot in my stomach every time schools were brought up or my gender was mentioned. Until that awful meeting, I'd been so happy with myself, but now I didn't want to think about it. I just wanted to exist, without feeling terrible.

'But it would be nice to stay with Ash, wouldn't it, darling?' Mum asked me. 'It would be nice to have someone you already know at St Joseph's?'

I shrugged. 'I'd have Daisy if I went to Queen Elizabeth's. I'd have a friend with me either way.' I put my eyes back towards the screen, wishing Mum would go away.

Instead, Mum did one of her long blinks where's she's collecting herself together so she doesn't raise her voice. 'I was thinking,' she said, 'that maybe, for the interests of getting into a school – and the one you prefer – you could just . . . pick a side. Pick what you want to be legally. For the paperwork, nothing else. Mrs Bailey said it would just be for the register, it doesn't have to be anything more than that.'

'Paperwork is official,' I said. 'I'd be saying, on a legal document, that I'm a boy or a girl. That's not what I am.'

'It wouldn't be real,' she insisted. 'We'd all know the truth, and we'd all believe you.'

'But I'll be stuck with that for another seven years. And it'll be a lie.' I looked at Ash. 'Did you know that even when I'm eighteen I won't be able to change my birth certificate to non-binary? It's not an option.'

Ash's nostrils widened. 'Really?'

'Yeah, you have to choose—'

'Jamie, please don't turn this into one of those arguments where you throw facts at me,' Mum said, clicking her fingers to get my attention. 'I'm not trying to pick a fight, I'm trying to help you. The local authority is being generous here. They're going to let you choose whether you want to put M or F on your forms, without needing a doctor's note. You just need to decide which school you like the best and we'll—'

'I'm not going to lie about who I am!' I stood up, bristling with anger like a cat. My controller crashed onto the carpet where it lay flashing in distress. 'I'm sick of it. I'm sick of being made to *choose* all the time – which toilets or changing rooms to use, or which side of the shop to get clothes from. I don't want to choose! I'm me, and I shouldn't change for the world. The world should change for me.'

Mum glared at me. 'I think that's an incredibly selfish thing to say, Jamie Rambeau.'

I glared back, my face full of hot pressure and my throat full of spikes. 'I'm not the only non-binary kid in the world, Mum. And none of us should have to lie about who we are just to make things easier for the rest of you.'

I stormed upstairs, leaving poor Ash sitting on the living room floor with my angry and upset mother standing next to him.

After that, things went from bad to worse.

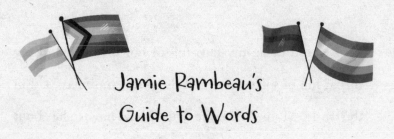

Jamie Rambeau's Guide to Words

Misgendering

Misgendering is when you refer to someone as a gender they're not. It would be like me calling Ash a girl, or sayng 'he' when I talked about Daisy. For me, misgendering is when someone refers to me as a boy or a girl, because I'm neither.

Misgendering can be very hurtful and make the person you're talking to or about really sad. If you do it by accident, apologise and try again.

6

Looking back, I think that if I'd had someone genuinely on my side trying to find a solution, I would have eventually given in and worked out how to carve out a place for myself in a binary school. But it felt like no one was even trying, or taking into account how I felt – they just wanted me to make a decision quickly. And I couldn't. So instead, I lay in bed that night absolutely prickling all over like I was covered in popping candy and I was in a paddling pool full of fizzy Vimto. I didn't want to choose. And I wasn't going to.

I was going to show the world that I deserved a place of my own in it.

I needed a plan of action.

Plans of Action are Daisy's speciality, but she spends every Sunday at Church Group, so the morning after my fight with Mum, Ash and me made a list of what we wanted to accomplish so Daisy would have something to go on when we saw her on Monday. We went to Ash's house to make the list because over breakfast Mum had tried again to get me interested in St Joseph's school, but I put the leaflets she'd printed straight into the recycling without looking at them, which only caused a row about wasting paper. I wasn't going to say sorry until she said sorry to me first. There was no chance of that happening EVER, so Ash's house became Action Plan Base Camp.

Ash's mum, Sana, is great. She bought me my first non-binary Pride badge when I told her about not being a girl or a boy, and she's never once forgotten what my pronouns are. She's always busy with a thousand different projects, but she will drop everything for her kids or their friends. That day, she nodded approvingly when we told her we were making a list of demands for the school, and told us she would keep us fuelled with snacks.

'You've got to be clear about what you want,' she said firmly, but kindly. 'Aim high. It's what you deserve. You, and anyone else who might be affected, of course,' she added.

So, armed with Ash's best felt-tip pens, a stack of printer paper and a plate full of spirally jalebi from his mum, we tried to work out exactly what it was we wanted. I had a lot of ideas, and we managed to get them down to five big points. I thought that it was a pretty good list.

OUR DEMANDS

Ash doesn't like the word demands but I overruled him

1. FOR GENDER MARKERS TO BE TAKEN OFF SCHOOL-
CHOICE FORMS

2. **OR** FOR NON-BINARY TO BE AN OPTION
(WE ARE WILLING TO NEGOTIATE)

3. FOR QE AND SJ SCHOOLS TO LOSE THEIR
'FOR GIRLS/BOYS' TITLES

4. FOR GENDER NEUTRAL TOILETS AND CHANGING
ROOMS TO BE IN ALL SCHOOLS

5. UNIFORM LISTS NOT TO BE SEPARATED
INTO BOYS AND GIRLS

I wanted to put more into it, get into things like pronouns
and stuff, but Ash pointed out that we should do these big
things first then work on the smaller things later. He said
then it would be easier, because there'd be a *precedent*.

A precedent means once people have said yes to something, you can use that to get them to say yes *again* when you ask them for other things. I got so excited about the demands that I wanted to just send the list to both head teachers that morning, but Ash managed to stop me.

'You can't just drop the demands out of the blue,' he said seriously. 'We need a campaign. We need to raise awareness of the problem, and then tell everyone what we want them to do to solve it.' Ash knows a lot about this sort of thing because his Auntie Mina is a local councillor and is always campaigning for various things.

The problem was, we weren't sure how to do a campaign of our own. We couldn't afford to print a lot of leaflets, Ash would never have been OK with knocking on doors, and neither of us knew how to build a website.

Luckily, Daisy had plenty of ideas.

'You need to make a big statement,' she said, skipping

to school on Monday. 'Get everyone's attention.' She thought for a moment. 'Without swearing at anyone, this time.'

'I can do that,' I said. 'How big of a big statement do you think we need to make? Should I go on hunger strike?' My stomach growled at the very idea.

'I don't think you're capable of going on hunger strike,' Daisy said reasonably. This was true. According to Mum and Dad, between Olly and me we managed to eat an entire bakery's worth of bread a week. Dad once caught Olly eating the emergency frozen bread straight from the freezer, a chunk at a time. He claimed it was like cold toast. 'Maybe a poster campaign?' Daisy suggested. 'We could stick them up around school, and convince people to write letters of support! Imagine a great huge sack of letters landing on Mrs Bailey's desk, all telling her she needs to do better.'

It was a nice thought. 'Let's do it,' I said. 'We'll stick

as many posters up as we can, so no one can ignore us.'

Ash brightened up at this. He's great at art. 'I can design the posters. And my uncle has a photocopier in his shop, he'd let me use it.'

'This is a great idea,' I said, practically bouncing into the classroom. 'We can tell everyone how non-binary kids are being forgotten about and need their help. We can paper the school!'

So at break time we sat down and started sketching out ideas for Ash to work into his design. He's got fancy software on his computer at home because his brother is a graphic designer, but we all worked on the ideas. It was hard to get everything we wanted to say onto a poster. It looked good just having *Non-Binary Rights!* in big bold letters, but that wasn't specific enough – people wouldn't know exactly what we were asking for.

'Maybe we can use your demands list,' Daisy said. 'One poster for each demand. That way people will know what changes we want.'

We ended up using all of the scrap paper out of the tray in the classroom, which didn't go down well with Miss Palanska when we were found out. 'That paper is for *everyone* to use,' she complained, but her expression softened slightly when she saw what we were drawing. 'Just make sure to leave some for the next person in future,' she said, before giving me a smile.

Despite the small telling-off, we managed to get everything written down and sketched, in the end. I was particularly proud of my illustrations of Mrs Bailey and Mr Dean, both of whom had frowny faces and stink-lines coming from their bums. Ash said he'd have to leave the stink lines out on the real posters, but I still have the originals in case they're ever needed.

'I think we've done a great job,' Daisy said, as we decided on the final ideas for the designs. 'Everyone will read the posters and know we mean business. They'll want to help and support you, I just know it.' She gave me a sideways hug. 'It's weird, because this is fun, but we shouldn't have to do it.'

'I know. I hope it works,' I said. 'If enough people learn about the school situation and get annoyed about it and write letters to complain, then the head teachers will have to listen. Won't they?'

*

The posters looked amazing. Super professional. Ash had outdone himself. They were yellow, white, purple and black – the colours of the non-binary flag – and they were definitely eye-catching. I was disappointed to see he'd left off my illustrations of the teachers altogether, but he'd done such a great job on the lettering that I couldn't get mad.

I felt nervous going into school with the posters. So far I'd done all my asking for change behind a closed office door. This was a big statement to make, and it felt like I was turning a spotlight onto myself. But if me and my friends didn't say something, who else would? I'd learnt that I wasn't even an afterthought for most people. I couldn't sit silently and expect anyone else to get angry on my behalf, could I?

I thumbed at the brand new packet of Blu-Tack that I'd swiped from the messy drawer in the kitchen. My mouth felt dry as we shared the posters between the three of us ready to decorate the walls.

We'd only stuck one poster up when Ms Lovell rounded the corner like a bull in Pamplona, ready to trample anyone in her path. I genuinely didn't think she'd have an issue because last year she'd let Jessica Hayworth stick up a million billion posters about her lost cat, and I thought that this was more important than a cat.

As usual, I was dead wrong.

She doesn't often shout, Ms Lovell, but when she

does she can reach inhuman volume that melts the wax out of your ears. Her voice was so loud her words got lost in the avalanche of sound. I know she said something about the walls having just been painted and who did we think we were and this really wasn't acceptable and she expected better of all of us but Ash especially.

'You usually let people put posters up,' I managed to say when she paused for breath.

'If they *ask* first,' she thundered. 'And if they're not about sensitive issues.' Then the shouting began again. To cut a long, loud story short, Ms Lovell told us we weren't allowed to put posters on the hall walls, or the noticeboards, or the stage, or in the toilets, or in the cloakroom, or on the doors. Which didn't leave us with much space.

'But we need people to see them!' I wailed. I was trying not to think about the fact she'd called this a *sensitive issue*. As she was the one shouting, it seemed to me like she was the one being sensitive. I didn't say that out loud, of course, because I was worried she might actually explode.

'Jamie, you haven't asked permission, and that amount of paper is a fire hazard,' she said, glaring at the ream of paper in Ash's arms. 'I know you're upset about this, but making a huge fuss is not the solution.' Then she turned on her heel and stormed off.

I stared after her, my heart thudding in my ears as I clung tightly to the beautiful posters we had spent so long making. I felt small and stupid.

Daisy put her arm around me. 'Are you OK?'

'I'm always OK,' I said, forcing a fake smile. 'Let's get these put up where we're allowed.'

The only place Ms Lovell hadn't explicitly banned was the library, so we stuck up as many of them as we could during break, taking care not to cover up the books. Miss Palanska let me put one up on the class noticeboard, and I also stuck a handful onto the lunch tables, but after lunch the dinner ladies picked them up and binned them so they could wipe the surfaces. I don't even know how many people actually saw the posters in the end, because even the ones in the library had disappeared the next day, and the caretaker had put a bus timetable up over the one in Palanska's room.

'I can't believe they've got rid of them all,' I said, moping outside at break time. I felt like a balloon with most of the air let out of it – just a saggy bag of breath left on the ground. I hadn't expected a non-binary revolution overnight, but I hadn't thought everything we had done would just be swept away and ignored either. 'That was a complete waste of time.'

'And ink,' Ash said, gloomily. 'And a Saturday. I had to promise my Uncle Arjun I'd work in the shop to pay for using the photocopier so much.' He pulled an incredibly glum face. 'Maybe we should rethink the plan.'

Daisy was making some of the posters we still had into

origami fortune-tellers. 'Don't get too down,' she said. 'That was only Plan A. There's loads more we can do. Maybe we need to think bigger than the school. Do something where Lovell can't exercise her authority.' She finished the fortune-teller and started writing numbers on the flaps in marker pen.

'What, like sticking posters up at Holly Hill Primary?' I asked. I couldn't imagine they'd be happy about that. There was a rumour their head teacher had a baseball bat wrapped in barbed wire under his desk, and the teachers had to wear riot gear on sports days.

'No, bigger than *any* school,' Daisy said.

My stomach clenched. 'I don't know,' I said, remembering Ms Lovell's words. 'I don't want to make a huge fuss. This isn't worth getting into serious trouble over.'

Ash gave me a quizzical look. 'Isn't it?' he asked.

I didn't know what to say to that.

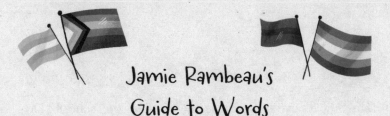

Jamie Rambeau's
Guide to Words

Pronouns

Pronouns are the words people use when talking about other people or words to use in place of their names. Pronouns can be words like he, she, they or it, but there are new pronouns being invented all the time, like e, xi or ze.

Using the wrong pronouns for someone is really rude, so if you do it by accident, you should say sorry and try not to do it again. Some people like one set of pronouns and stick to them forever, but other people change theirs sometimes. Either way is fine!

My pronouns are they/them/theirs.

What are yours?

7

It was October half term. Daisy, Ash and I had ended up at Yeoman Park, because there's literally nowhere else to go in our tiny town, sitting on the top of the tallest half-pipe at the skate park. Plenty of people use the skate park but no one skates or bikes on the big half-pipe to skate or bike on. The older kids call it 'The Cheesegrater' because if you fall on it, it takes your skin clean off. Instead, it gets used to sit on.

Daisy and Ash were chatting about something. I wasn't listening. I was kicking my heels hard on the wood beneath me and wondering whether, if you had enough cling film, you could wrap it around and around the structure and create sides so when it rained you'd have made a really deep swimming pool with clear walls on either side.

Someone nudged me. 'What?' I asked.

'We said, do you want to go to Ben's Bakery and get a sandwich?' Daisy asked. When I didn't respond right away, she huffed. 'What's up with you?'

'Gee, I don't know,' I said flatly. 'Maybe the fact that my teachers, current and future, are trying their hardest to pretend I don't exist, my parents wish I was someone else and when I tried to make a difference it didn't work.' The deadline for applying to secondary schools was upon us. Whilst Ash and Daisy had their applications in, I'd been granted an extension due to 'exceptional circumstances', but the options were still the same – the school for girls, or the school for boys.

'Yeah, maybe it's all that,' Ash said.

Daisy sighed. 'It's half term! Come on, let's do something fun. We can see if the Hallowe'en shop is still open!'

That got my attention. It was Hallowe'en in two nights. On our high street is a shop that's almost always empty except for two instances a year – Hallowe'en and Christmas time. It sells really awful stuff, but at £1 an item, it's the must-go-to place for anyone on pocket-money wages.

'Sure.' I stood up. 'I'll see if they've got any goth makeup for Olly.' We went down the ladder and crossed the skate park quickly to avoid being mown down by the maniacs on their BMX bikes.

The high street was a bit busier than usual, but we got into the Hallowe'en shop OK and mingled in with the other dozen people who'd crammed themselves inside looking for costumes or face paint. We always go trick-or-treating as a trio, though I suddenly wondered whether this would be the last year we did it.

I already had my costume planned out. I was going to go as the Mandalorian (I was borrowing Olly's costume from a couple of years ago) because he wears a suit that covers him completely and the costume makes you utterly unknowable. Daisy was recycling her zombie bride outfit from last year, and Ash's mum had made him a duck costume. If Ash hadn't been our best friend, Daisy and I would have laughed ourselves stupid at the idea of a duck costume, but Ash loves ducks, so we were going along with it, even if we were going to look weird walking down the road together.

I picked up some black and white makeup to gift for Olly as Daisy paid for a zombie face paint pack and Ash wondered aloud whether he'd get in trouble for buying a water pistol that was disguised as a packet of chewing gum.

Everything felt normal, and the big ball of anxiety in my stomach started to unravel, just a little bit.

We wandered out into the October sunshine, and I watched the leaves skitter across the pavement like a group of brown mice. It felt nice to have a week with no school and a bit of normality where we could just be the three of us again. I linked my arms through Ash's and Daisy's, one on either side, and we walked along, taking up most of the pavement and getting on people's nerves.

'We'll have to walk down the corridors like this next year,' I said, then realised. 'Or . . . not.'

Ash gave a weak laugh. 'If we're going to be doing that, we'll need longer arms.'

'Yeah,' Daisy said, unlinking from me. 'About a mile long each.'

The mood came crashing down like a piano dropped off a roof. That was the problem with reality, I thought bitterly. It kept on rolling away in the background without you noticing like some sort of horrible steamroller until it was close enough to squish you flat without you even having noticed.

'UGH!' I threw my arms into the air. 'This SUCKS!'

'Sucks sour lemons with salt on top,' Daisy agreed. Then she gave a sort of resigned shrug. 'Look,' she said. 'I know what'll happen, and I'll be alright with it eventually, I guess.'

I blinked. 'What do you mean? What's going to happen?'

Daisy stared at me. 'You'll go to Ash's school, won't you.' It didn't sound like a question, and it caught me unexpectedly between the ribs.

'I don't know,' I said, feeling like I was lying. But I wasn't. I really didn't know. 'I've not decided. I don't want to just . . . follow Ash because he needs me.'

'Hey,' Ash said, clearly put out. 'I don't need babying, Jamie. I'm not a useless kid.' He glowered, nostrils reduced to slits. I'd touched a nerve and knew I had to start back-pedalling.

'I didn't say you were useless,' I said. 'I . . . Come on, this isn't important right now, is it?' I looked around desperately. 'We're having fun, aren't we?'

'Yeah, we are,' Daisy said. 'But every time we have fun together is one step closer to being the *last* fun time we have together. I don't want to not be able to do this on a random afternoon. It isn't fair.'

'You think *that's* not fair?' I snorted, feeling slightly aggravated.

Daisy folded her arms. 'I don't know, Jamie. You've had your head in the clouds all week, worrying about yourself. But it doesn't seem like you've thought about what this means to me and Ash. We're being split up, whatever *you* decide. Ash is my best friend, same as you, and we don't even have the option of going to the same school. That's not fair either, right, Ash?'

'Right,' Ash agreed. 'I – I don't want to leave Daisy. There's nothing any of us can do to stop it happening, though. Whichever school you choose, Jamie, you can't have us both, but at least you get to have one of us. Have you thought about how sad *we* are? One of us is going to be alone.'

I stopped, my mouth flapping like a goldfish out of the bowl. I wanted to say that it wasn't the same for them, that they were going to schools where their gender wasn't being questioned and that made the blow of being split up easier to handle . . . but did it? Had I not noticed how this was hurting Daisy and Ash as well? I shut my mouth and felt myself going extremely red. Maybe I had been selfish.

Ash scuffed his shoe on the pavement. 'We don't know what it's like to be you, Jamie, but we do know what it's like to be losing friends.'

'It's not just losing friends, though!' I snapped,

embarrassment and sadness making me sound angry. 'What I've got going on, it's more important than that!' That was both true and not true at the same time, and I hated myself for saying it, but also I felt like I had the perfect right to shout it as much as I wanted.

Unfortunately, it went down like a lead balloon.

Daisy glared at me. 'You're more important than your friends?' It was the sort of dangerous question that there's no right answer to. It was a diving-board question – you jump off it into deep water regardless.

I folded my arms in a huff. I didn't want to explain. I'd had enough of explaining. I never wanted to have to explain myself ever again in my whole entire life. It was too tangled-up and none of it was my fault.

Daisy clicked her tongue. 'You're not the most important person in this group, Jamie. We've all got problems and we're all worried about next year. You're not even the one who's got it the worst!'

'What?!' I exploded. 'You think you have it worse than me?'

'It's not a competition,' Ash muttered.

But Daisy's eyes flashed. 'At the end of all this, Jamie, you get to *choose*. It might not be what you want, but you get to choose where you go. Me and Ash just have to go where we're sent, whether we like it or not. We can't change who we are any more than you can!'

'But that's the whole point!' I said. 'You don't *have* to change who you are. Or lie about it, for some stupid form.'

Daisy shook her head. 'You don't get it. You really don't get it.'

'You're right,' I snapped. 'I don't get it. Having a strop because you can't pick your school!'

She stared at me. 'It's not the school I'm bothered about,' she said, quieter than before. 'It's Ash and you. You'll go to Ash's school and then you'll have each other, while I lose both of my best friends. But you don't seem to be thinking about anyone except yourself.'

'I'm thinking about everyone I can!' I snapped back, though it didn't feel truthful.

'I don't know if you are, Jamie. It feels — it feels like I'm losing you already. You've not asked Ash or me how we feel about being split up. It's like you've forgotten this is happening to all of us.'

'Can you blame me?' I snapped. 'I've got *real* problems!'

She huffed out a humourless laugh. 'Wow. **OK.** I didn't realise I was friends with someone quite so selfish.'

It felt like she'd thumped me. I took a step backwards, and Ash looked at the ground.

Daisy shook her head. 'I'm going home.'

'I'll come with you,' Ash said, to my surprise.

I stood there and watched them walk away, and I suddenly understood what Daisy had been saying. I had been so busy worrying about schools, I'd forgotten to worry about my friends. And now there was the chance that I really had lost them forever.

Jamie Rambeau's Guide to Words

Gender Dysphoria

When you are born, the midwife or the doctor decides whether you're a boy or a girl based on the way your body looks. But for some people, looks can be deceiving and they're given the wrong gender.

Gender dysphoria is the uncomfortable feeling some people get when their true gender is different from the one they were given at birth.

No matter how someone's body looks, they might identify as male, female, non-binary, or another label altogether. The important thing to remember is to listen when people tell you about themselves, and to be kind and caring.

Gender Euphoria

This is the opposite! **Gender euphoria** is the happy feeling people get instead of gender dysphoria. A trans or non-binary person might feel gender euphoria by wearing clothes that mean they are presenting as their true gender, or by someone using their correct pronouns. Cisgender people feel gender euphoria too – when they feel good in a snazzy suit or with a new haircut, or when someone gives them a great compliment about themselves.

I get a lot of gender euphoria when someone talks about me using they/them pronouns!

What gives you gender euphoria?

8

So, that had been a disaster.

After my fight with Daisy and Ash, I had big plans to lie down on my bed and just wait for death. Unfortunately, my parents have this uncanny ability to spot when something bad has happened to me and begin a process called Take Your Mind Off It, which is code for Give Jamie Chores. It could have been worse, and I guess it did take my mind off the fact that Daisy and Ash weren't speaking to me, but after a day of washing the cars and dusting the surfaces and cleaning the oven I was aching all over and exhausted.

'That's what a day's real work does to you,' Dad said briskly, as if I usually spend all my time being fanned by servants and fed peeled grapes. He ruffled my hair. 'How're you feeling?'

'Like I've gone ten rounds with a monster truck,' I said. Then shrugged. 'OK, I guess.'

'They'll get over themselves. You're too good friends for it to last forever.'

He was probably right, but I still felt like hot garbage. It was Hallowe'en, and since I hadn't messaged Daisy or Ash and they hadn't messaged me either, it meant our trick-or-treating was probably cancelled. It was going to be our last one, as well. I sank into the sofa and wished the cushions would consume me.

'Oliver!' I heard Mum yell from upstairs. 'What were you thinking?!'

I rolled my eyes, wondering what he'd been caught

doing this time. I didn't have to wait long to find out. Olly came downstairs carrying the laundry basket and wearing a stupid grin. 'What did you do?' I asked.

His grin widened. 'Well, you know that witchy skirt mum never wears anymore, with all the lace and fluffy bits?'

'Oh no,' I groaned. 'You didn't cut it up and make something with it, did you?'

'Of course not, I'm not an animal,' he gasped. 'I wore it out last night, that's all.'

'Ah.' I sat back and let Olly drag the basket into the kitchen as Mum followed him, screeching about boundaries and thieving. I'd love to have Olly's problems, sometimes. All of his are self-inflicted.

He came back into the living room once the washer was spinning and flopped next to me. Then he looked me up and down, before folding his arms dramatically and scowling. I looked down at my own crossed arms and realised he was copying me.

'Oh, ha ha, very funny,' I said, uncrossing my arms just long enough to throw a pillow at him.

'What's up with you?' he asked. 'School's out, you should be happy. What's going on?'

I told him about Daisy and Ash and the falling-out.

He let me tell the story without interrupting. Then, once I'd finished, he gave a huge sigh. 'OK,' he said, unfolding himself. 'You're all idiots.'

'Thanks.' I snorted.

'I'm being serious. You are. But! It's kind of understandable because you've all got a lot going on. None of you are wrong, and none of you are exactly in the right, either.'

I stared at him. 'It's not that I'm not thinking about us all being split up,' I said. 'But it's like . . . that's happening to me *as well as* my other stuff.'

'I get that,' he said. 'The thing is, Daisy and Ash

love you so much that they can't imagine there ever being a bigger problem than the three of you not being together. The knowledge that you're going to be split up one way or another has probably been eating them alive for weeks, Jamie.'

That made sense. 'Why didn't they talk to me about it though?'

He laughed. 'Oh, Jamie, come on. You were almost levitating with rage at having to choose between schools, why would they try to give you *more* things to worry about? They probably thought you'd realise they had things they were worried about too. Eventually.'

'It's not like I forgot about them,' I said. 'We've still been hanging out and they helped me do the posters and . . .' I trailed off. 'Oh,' I said, realising. 'That was just for *my* problem.'

'Mm-hm.' Olly checked his nails. 'Now, let's get one thing straight – or not so straight, given who's talking here. But let's get something clear, OK? You're allowed to want a school that accepts you for who you are and doesn't expect you to lie or change. That's fine. But . . .'

'But I need to lose the tunnel vision?' I asked. 'Make sure Daisy and Ash aren't just my . . . lackeys?'

'Precisely.' Olly smiled. 'I know you'll be best friends again in a few days and when you are, just remember that you're a team, not Jamie Rambeau and their followers, yeah?'

I blushed. 'Yeah, I know.' I prodded him. 'Thanks.'

'I'm so wise,' Olly said modestly. 'It's frankly a mystery why I don't have my own advice column in a magazine. Now, are you going to come and help with my Hallowe'en costume?'

Olly's costume turned out to be Elvira, the goth lady with a big beehive of black hair and a skin-tight dress. He needed my help getting into it, and then I had to stand there holding the mirror close whilst he painted his face.

'What on *Earth* do you look like?' Mum asked as she passed the bedroom door.

'Like the most beautiful woman in the world,' Olly said, without missing a beat. He blew her a kiss in the mirror and she smiled, pretending to catch it.

'You'll catch your death,' she said, but without much malice. The skirt incident was clearly forgotten. 'Jamie, are you going out?'

'I don't think so,' I said. 'They haven't messaged me. Think I'll just stay in and watch *Hocus Pocus*.'

'If that's what you're doing I might stay in too,' Olly said, though he carried on applying lipstick. 'Love Bette Midler.'

Mum whisked me away then and put me in charge of making popcorn and slicing up hot dog rolls for tea. She never normally bothers with a big Hallowe'en tea, and I knew she was only doing it now because I wasn't going out. It somehow made me feel better and worse at the same time.

Olly left shortly after that, tottering out of the house in heels and promising to be back before midnight in case he turned into a pumpkin. My parents and I squashed up on the sofa and watched the Sanderson Sisters begin their evil deeds on DVD.

We'd only just got to the bit where they turn the boy into the cat when there was a knock at the door. Dad groaned – he'd lost the coin toss, so he had to answer the door to trick-or-treaters. I heard him open the door and make a few sounds of surprise, and when he came back in, he was trailed by a blue zombie bride and someone covered in feathers and foam and wearing a baseball cap painted to look like a duck's head.

'Why aren't you dressed?' the zombie bride asked, holding up her empty bucket.

I gawped at her.

The duck pushed his duck cap up. 'Number Eleven Long Meadow Lane is giving out full-size Snickers!'

I looked back and forth between Daisy and Ash 'But . . .' I tried to remember how to talk. My heart felt as if it had swollen up so quickly and so much that it now took up my entire ribcage. I wanted to cry and scream and hug them and laugh all at once. 'But I thought we were—'

'Oh come on.' Daisy grinned. 'It was only an argument. A stupid one. This could be our last Hallowe'en. Are you coming or not?'

'Two minutes,' I said, and flew up the stairs to get changed. I crashed back down again as fast as I could, now wrapped in armour and carrying a helmet under my arm.

'That's more like it.' Mum beamed at me. 'You have fun, won't you? Be back before eight, you've got school the day after next.'

We spilled out into the street and Daisy took my arm as we headed off towards the big houses at the end of the estate.

'Sorry,' she said. 'I was mean.'

'No you weren't,' I said. 'I was. Or maybe we both were. Or weren't. I'm sorry, anyway.'

'We all have different worries,' Ash concluded, consulting the map on his phone. 'Doesn't mean one is more or less important than another. And we're all thinking about next year. It's going to be pants for everyone.' That was a big speech, for Ash. I wondered if he'd been practising it.

'I do get that you've got extra worries no one else in school has,' Daisy continued. 'But that doesn't mean me and Ash are fine, you know?'

'I know,' I said.

'Maybe if we get the head teachers to stop being so up themselves, everyone will win? We could even have combined PE or something. Which could benefit everyone, eventually.'

'I hope so,' I said as we got to Long Meadow Lane. 'This isn't just about me. It's not the Jamie Rambeau Show.'

'Isn't it?' Daisy laughed and looked around as if trying to spot the cameras, then her face became serious. 'Maybe it *should* be, though? We could try and get you on the radio or TV or something.'

'I don't think they let just anyone on the television, Daisy,' Ash said. 'We're at school all day. We're already in trouble about the posters. And—'

'It was only an idea, keep your hair on.'

'Daisy's right, though,' I said, feeling reinflated by her enthusiasm. 'We need to tell people who aren't in the school. The people in charge of the big decisions. Like . . . the government.' We all pulled identical faces of disgust. 'OK, maybe not them, but how about whoever's in charge of school admissions? The council maybe. They've probably never thought about how binary forms and schools hurt some people. We could be their wake-up call. We could do it not just for me, but for all the non-binary kids who will come in the future!'

Ash had started sweating, nostrils flared. 'That sounds like a big deal.'

'*I'm* a big deal,' I said, though I didn't feel like it. 'But you don't have to join in with anything you don't want to.'

'I want to help you, though,' he said. 'What's more important than a best friend?' He looked away quickly, his ears deep red.

I smiled but my chest hurt. I'd never thought there might be a future where I didn't have Ash and Daisy together. It was a world I didn't want, but it was coming anyway. Maybe I'd manage to change the way schools treated non-binary people one day – but I would still lose either Daisy or Ash. It felt really unfair. Growing up was bad and change was worse. I wanted to press pause on everything, just to keep my friends, both of my friends, with me for as long as I could.

But there's no pause button in real life. So I put my arms around both of them at once, and pulled them into a group hug.

'Thank you,' I said. 'I mean it.'

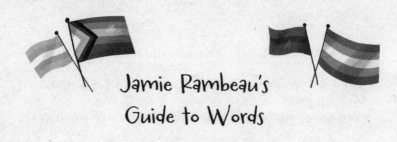

Jamie Rambeau's
Guide to Words

Coming Out

Coming out usually means telling people about your gender or sexuality (something that straight and cisgender people don't have to do). There's no right or wrong way to feel about doing this – for some people it's a huge deal, but for others it's just another ordinary day. Some people never come out, and no one should be pressured into it if they don't want to.

The phrase '**coming out**' was copied from the 'coming out' into high society that posh young ladies called debutantes used to do when they attended their first big party. Some LGBTQ people used to have their own big debutante-style balls as well! I bet Olly would have loved to go to one of those . . .

Coming out is often not something an LGBTQ person has to do just the once – it's every time you meet someone new, move to a new place, or get a new job. Doing this over and over again can be exhausting. It's also a personal thing – you should never tell people about someone's gender or sexuality if they haven't given you permission to do so.

9

When people hear that you're trans or non-binary, they put on a sympathetic face. 'Poor you,' they say. 'It must be very difficult.'

Actually, being non-binary is great. It's one of the things I like best about myself. I like that I was born this way, and it gives me a happy feeling when someone calls me 'them' when they talk about me. And it can be very easy to just get on and live happily, as long as everyone treats me like a person. It's only other people who make being transgender difficult at all.

Being trans could be a joyous thing. We could celebrate people discovering themselves, we could have coming-out parties and gender reveal cakes for teenagers and adults as well – congratulations, they're non-binary! I'd love to cut into a cake and it have four layers of different coloured sponge and have everyone agree what a wonderful thing it is.

But we don't. They don't.

I keep saying it: being trans is fine, it's the world that's the problem. And that's what people don't seem to get. There are loads of us as well. Whether you make room for us or not, whether you accept us or not, whether you include us or not, we're still going to be here. And us existing doesn't take anything away from you, or make your life more difficult. Making space for me doesn't mean you have to give up your seat.

Some people seem to think that if they don't give us a space, we'll stop existing. They'd like us to be denied access to toilets or doctors' appointments or correct pronouns on forms. They hope that if they could do all that, we might decide to go away. Even though nothing we're doing is hurting them, they wish we didn't exist.

Being my true self is easy.

I wish other people could see that.

*

We decided that we would go to the local council building and talk to whoever was in charge about this problem with the school system. Explain to them that I was getting left out of the process. I didn't tell my parents our plan, of course; I knew they were too stressed about missing the main application deadline to think my idea was a good one. I did tell my brother about it, though.

'Love it,' Olly said as he put eyeliner on. 'Loved the idea of a big statement with the posters, but I love the idea of talking to the man in charge, too.'

'It might not be a man,' I pointed out.

He tutted at me. 'I mean the *metaphorical* Man. The one ruining the environment and poisoning the whales. The Man. The one you stick it to.' He looked at me in the mirror. 'You OK? You've been like a ghost recently. Didn't you make up with Daisy and Ash?'

'Yeah, I did. It's everything else.' I gestured around at nothing in particular. 'I don't want to make a fuss, but—'

'Hold up.' Olly raised a black-nail-varnished hand. '*Why* don't you want to make a fuss?'

'Because I don't want to get in trouble. Or lose the limited options I *do* have.' I fiddled with Olly's *Golden Girls* bedsheets. 'I'm not being a wimp.'

'Never said you were, Jamie. But sometimes . . .' He sighed, and turned to look at me properly. 'Sometimes you have to make a fuss,' he said, without his usual flippant tone. 'What do you think Pride is all about?'

'Isn't it a big party?' I asked, thinking of the pictures

I'd seen online of banners and parades and people covered in glitter and rainbows. It looked good fun.

Olly shook his head. 'It's much more than that. It's a big celebration, yes, but Pride started at an LGBTQ bar in New York. The place was called the Stonewall Inn – and it was somewhere that should have been a safe space for LGBTQ people – but the cops threw them out and arrested them because, amongst other reasons, they were seen as not wearing the right clothes for their gender.' He paused, and looked at his makeup table for an instant. 'That happened all the time, but on one particular night, the people there fought back and eventually rioted over the course of a few days. LGBTQ people started gathering at Stonewall to spread the word about activism. And a year later, the first Pride march set off from the Stonewall Inn.' He stared at me. 'The first Pride wasn't a party, it was a protest. It was queer people protesting because they were being targeted for no good reason.'

I couldn't think of anything to say. I had no idea. Why had no one ever told me that before?

Olly shrugged again. 'Pride is now a party *and* a big protest. Always has been, and it still is among the glitter and rainbows. Give it a Google, little sibling. I know that you're worried about getting into trouble. I know you're not like me, you're a good kid. But sometimes . . . sometimes making a fuss is what you have to do to get listened to. Maybe you'll get into a bit of trouble but if it changes something, won't that be worth it?' He turned back to the mirror and picked up his black lipstick. 'Do you want me to go into town with you?'

'Thanks,' I said, my head full of heavy thoughts, 'but I think we'll be OK.'

'Please yourself. I'm at the other end of the phone if you do need me, any time.' He stood up, came over to me and before I could protest, smacked a big lipstick kiss on my cheek.

'Gerroff.' I shoved him away and wiped my cheek. Black coated the back of my hand. 'Ugh, you're disgusting.'

'Love you too.' He laughed. 'And good luck. Make a fuss, I dare you.'

*

I did do some reading about Pride after Olly had gone. He was right, as usual. Pride wasn't just a big party, it was a protest as well as a celebration. Still, I didn't know if me, Daisy and Ash could pull off a big protest on our own.

We gathered at Ash's house again to discuss.

'What about asking for recognition of a special awareness day?' Sana, Ash's mum, suggested. We were all slumped on her sofa. 'Surely there's a non-binary people's day? The local council usually emails schools with details of their plans for days like those too.'

I sat up. 'That's a great idea, Mrs C. Let's check!'

I pulled my phone back out and Daisy and Ash crowded closer to see. We found out that International Non-Binary People's Day was on 14th July. That was months and months away, but it did give me another idea.

The Council House building in the centre of Nottingham is a great big fake-marble building that has been made to look like a miniature St Paul's Cathedral. Every year for Pride Month, it flies a bunch of rainbow flags from the flagpoles. They even drape the stone lions at the entrance in rainbow ribbons and it always looks great. So, I figured, why not ask them to fly a non-binary flag for my special day? It would be a great jumping-off point for discussing about the lack of inclusion in the local schools.

'I like it,' Daisy said. 'Decorating the building is something they already do, so there's that thing. Precedent. They just need a flag to fly. We can buy one online. Maybe we should ask them to decorate the lions and everything as well, like they do for Pride.'

'I don't know, I think we should ask for the flag and see how we get on with that first,' I said. Olly's words about making a fuss were rolling about in my mind, but I was still too nervous to ask for everything I wanted, even if other people already had it. 'But yeah, buy the flag, I'll give you the money for it.' Daisy has a debit card and is allowed to buy things online, but my parents (and Ash's) still hand over solid coins on pocket-money day.

The flag arrived the next day, so we decided to put our plan into action the following Saturday. I told my parents we were going into Notts to go to Waterstones, and was asked to be back by four. I didn't think we'd be in town for that long, but made a mental note to stay at Daisy's or Ash's house until the last possible moment if we got back early. I didn't want to come back before I had to; things were still awkward at home.

Ash really doesn't like going into the town centre

because he hates public transport, but we managed to get a seat with a table and a window on the train in, which made it better.

Daisy scrolled the council's website on her phone as we set off. 'They've not updated this since 2019,' she snorted, 'but there are some good photos of Pride. It looks like they really get into it!' She turned her phone towards me so I could see.

I scrolled through a few of the photos, which showed happy, smiling people, couples and families all wearing bright clothes and covered in bucketfuls of glitter. I'd never been to a Pride parade, but I made my mind up to go to the next one.

'There's nothing on the site about Pride being a protest as well as a party,' I said. 'I wonder if they know?'

'Maybe not,' Daisy said, taking her phone back. 'But they seem enthusiastic about Pride at any rate.' She excused herself to go to the toilet then, leaving me and Ash alone at the table. I pulled the council website up on my own phone, looking for information about how to get a flag approved for the flagpole, when I heard Ash do one of his deep breaths, and I knew a speech was coming.

'Jamie,' he said quietly, as though we were being spied on. 'Would . . . would you think about coming to St Joseph's with me?'

I looked up, surprised. This wasn't like Ash. Normally he coasted along with whatever everyone else wanted to do – asking for something was way out of his comfort zone, and he was blushing like mad. My heart did a horrible sort of clench. Because it would have been easy to say yes and reassure Ash that we were best mates and always would be, and that we'd go to secondary school together and everything would be fine. It would have made him happy. I wanted him to be happy.

But I couldn't lie to him.

'I don't know,' I said instead. 'I don't know what's going to happen.'

I expected him to shrug and say OK but instead he said, 'You want to go to school with Daisy, don't you?'

'Don't be like that,' I started.

'But you do,' he said, his voice shrinking to a little mouse-squeak. 'Everyone would rather be her friend than mine, it's obvious. I'd rather be her friend than mine, too. But – but Daisy will be fine making new friends, and I won't. I don't know how to make new friends. I've always had you two and I never needed anyone else.' He looked away and fished a tissue out his sleeve to wipe his nose crossly. 'I know it's a boys' school, but we'd be together and we could look after each other, couldn't we?'

I didn't know what to say.

At that moment, Daisy came back in, face screwed up is disgust. 'That toilet is so gross,' she said, taking hand gel out of her bag. 'Have you found out anything about the flagpole?'

'There's nothing online,' I said, covering for Ash, who was looking guiltily at his lap. 'I think we just need to be clear about it all, explain how difficult it is making a choice about school, and the fact it's going to be International Non-Binary People's Day in the summer and make our request. They'll be interested, I'm positive.'

We spent the rest of the journey playing HangNoughts in my notebook, though Ash clearly didn't have his heart in it, barely sighing when Daisy got his man hanged in less than a minute. Daisy didn't seem to notice the cloud of gloom hovering over Ash's head. Ash was right, Daisy was loud, funny and outgoing and everyone liked her.

I liked her.

And, as I sat watching them chatting about nothing in particular, my chest began to ache. Whatever happened, I was going to have to leave one of my best friends behind.

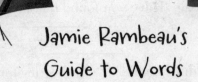

Jamie Rambeau's Guide to Words

LGBTQ

LGBTQ is an acronym – every letter stands for something:

L – Lesbian

G – Gay

B – Bisexual

T – Transgender

Q – Queer

Sometimes there's a + after it as well, because there are so many identities it would be a super-long acronym if we tried to squash them all in. Non-binary people come under the T for Transgender, because we don't identify with the gender we were assigned when we were born.

10

We walked through town feeling half like villains and half like secret agents. I had the folded-up non-binary flag in my backpack, and some print-outs about Non-Binary People's Day. Daisy had a backpack full of face paint ('In case we need to make a statement!'), and Ash had a lot of worries. He had worked himself up into a lather before we even got out of the train station.

'What if they throw us out?' he squeaked, holding his backpack so tight he looked in danger of absorbing it. 'What if we get in trouble?'

'We can't get in trouble for asking a question,' I said. 'I don't think. Besides, it's a public building, anyone's allowed in, aren't they?'

Daisy nodded. 'I think so. It'll be fine, Ash. Relax.'

Ash did not relax, and instead pulled his hood up and burrowed down into the neck of his clothes, to the point where he looked like a disembodied pair of eyes floating in the dark.

We had to walk from the station into the middle of town to get to the Council House. Ash has been nervous about crowds his whole life, so he made us take the long way to avoid the busy shopping centre. By the time we got to the town square, where the Council House building was, Daisy was cross, my feet were complaining *and* I needed the toilet.

This was a problem.

Public toilets are my nemeses. I've almost wet myself on multiple occasions because I've tried to hold it in rather than pick which one to use. Small coffee shops are usually the best places because they tend to have one toilet for everyone to share, but they often expect you to buy something. I don't like using disabled toilets because I'm not disabled and I might be in there when someone who actually needs to use the space wants to. Then there's the problem of finding a toilet at all – the Council closed the public ones in the centre down during the pandemic lockdown and never reopened them, so if you get caught out you've got to make a decision fast, or else end up sneaking into the cat café and hoping no one spots you slinking around the walls to get to the toilet.

'Go in McDonald's,' Daisy suggested. 'It's busy in there, no one will notice you've not bought anything. Though if you're buying, I wouldn't mind some chips.'

'They have separate men's and women's toilets in there,' I whined. 'What if someone stops me?'

Daisy took her pink baseball cap off and plonked it

on my head. 'There you go. Ta-da. Now you're a girl.'

'Wow,' I said, adjusting the hat. 'Master of disguise, you are. Is that all that's needed? A pink hat?'

'Or Ash could give you his blue jacket and you can pretend you're a boy, either way. People are stupid, and no one will bother you.'

'Amazing how little it takes to blend in with the general public, to be honest,' I said. 'I'll be right back.'

I went into the McDonald's, trying to look casual as I headed straight for the toilets. I used to love McDonald's, but last year Daisy bet me I couldn't finish twenty nuggets by myself. Well, I did manage, but the problem was they soon made a reappearance. I haven't been able to eat them since.

The smell made my stomach churn straight away. Fortunately, I had the loos to myself. Right until I started washing my hands that is, and a lady came in to put her lipstick on.

I saw her, in the mirror, look me up and down, very deliberately.

I'm tall for my age, I always have been. Mum and Dad are both tall, and Olly is six foot two in heels. I've got Dad's broad shoulders, but Mum's skinny face and hands. My clothes that day were baggy jeans and a *Dracula Death Mansion* t-shirt I got for pre-ordering the game, but with a denim jacket and Daisy's pink hat on as well. My clothes were mixed-up enough to be confusing, plus I had Daisy's pink hat. I was hoping that was enough to allow me to wash my hands in peace.

The woman with the lipstick looked at me again as I went to the hand dryers.

People don't usually stare at me. They glance, but that's about it. This woman was staring so hard I could pretty much feel her eyeballs pressing on my face. I kept drying my hands, waiting for the question I felt sure was coming. *Are you in the wrong room?* I'd have to say no even though the answer was technically yes and then what would happen? Why couldn't I just pee in peace and why did this even matter anyway?

'Excuse me?' she said, as I went for the door.

I looked around, ready to apologise, or run.

'I wanted to say – your jacket is *stunning*,' she said, beaming. 'I love all the badges on it, where did you get them from?'

'Oh!' Relieved, I looked at my jacket, which was covered in enamel pins. There was the non-binary flag one Ash's mum had given me, one with Grogu from *The Mandalorian* on it, another round one with 'I <3 Gummy Bears' on it that Daisy got me, and loads of others. 'I don't know. Just . . . places. I collect them.'

'Well, it's fabulous. Very eye-catching.' She smiled again, then turned back to the mirror.

My heart started again and I hurried out back into the thick chicken nugget haze before making it back outside.

Daisy and Ash were leaning on the wall over the train tracks, looking annoyed.

'Did you fall in?' Daisy asked, taking her hat back.

'No, I was washing my hands,' I said primly. 'Some of us do that, you know.'

'I wash my hands,' Ash said.

'I just lick mine clean,' Daisy said, with a wicked look at Ash, who pretended to heave. 'Come on, the Council House is down the next street.'

The Council House isn't actually a house, it's a huge brick building with a white stone front and two statues of lions guarding it. The lions are rubbish at their jobs, though – they let people climb on them all day. There's always a protest going on outside the building or someone handing out leaflets that tell you the end is nigh. They've been handing out the same leaflet since I was a little kid, so if the end *is* nigh, then 'nigh' must mean 'anytime between now and a million billion years into the future'.

Today there was a rainbow flag flying on one of the flagpoles next to the Union flag, and my spirits rose. It made me feel pretty good about our chances of getting our flag up there too.

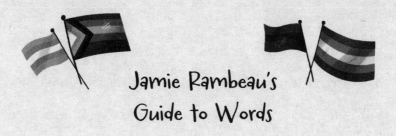

Jamie Rambeau's
Guide to Words

Courage

Courage is the choice and willingness to confront agony, pain, danger, uncertainty or intimidation.

To do something even if it scares you.

It can take courage to do something as wild as bungee jumping or as ordinary as being yourself.

11

Inside the Council House, it was noisier than I'd thought it would be. There were a lot of people standing around, not doing much. The air was that stale heat flavour that comes from poor air circulation and warm bodies. There was a big round desk in the centre of the room with two women at it, both of them on the phone and looking busy.

'Shall we go up and ask?' Daisy whispered.

'I guess.' There didn't seem to be a queue, and no one was holding a ticket or anything, so we just went straight up to the desk in a bunch. The woman closest gave us a quick smile and held up a finger to say *One minute, please* as she kept on talking into the phone.

Ash fidgeted as we waited, moving from foot to foot like he was standing on hot coals, whilst Daisy picked up a few information sheets that were on the desk. I looked around the room. It had a high ceiling, wood-panelled walls and a worn polished floor. There were two security guards chatting beside some doors that looked like they led deeper into the building and in the middle of the lobby, a few paces behind the desk, there was a big sweeping staircase that split in two on a slim landing, before carrying on upwards and out of sight.

I wondered what was up there.

'Now, then.' The woman put the phone down. 'How can I help you young people?'

Nerves suddenly took hold of me, but I made myself speak. This was my problem, after all. 'I was wondering, excuse me, sorry, if we could talk to the person in charge of the flags?' I asked.

'The flags?' She blinked, but not unkindly.

'On the flagpole,' I said, pointing up like she could see through the ceiling. 'We want to ask if we can put a flag up there.'

'Oh, I'm afraid you wouldn't be allowed to go up there,' she said, clearly not getting it.

'No.' I took the flag out of my backpack. 'I mean, I've got a flag, and I want it to be flown on Non-Binary Day.'

'On what day, sweetheart?'

I took one of the deep breaths Olly is always advising. 'In July,' I said, 'it's International Non-Binary People's Day. I would like the non-binary flag to fly over the city on that day. Can we talk to someone about it? Please.'

She gave a slow nod. 'I see. It's like Pride, is it?'

'Exactly,' Daisy said, breathing out in relief. 'You see, my friend Jamie has to choose between—'

'It's OK, Daisy, she doesn't need my life story.' I talked over her before she could derail the train of conversation entirely. 'We'd just like to know if this can be flown. Maybe. Please.'

The woman picked up her phone again. 'Let me give a call to Mr Whitbread. He's our community engagement lead.'

That sounded promising. We'd only been in the building for five minutes and we were getting to speak to someone in charge! Ash stopped looking quite so nervous, and Daisy looked rather pleased with our own success as the woman asked Mr Whitbread to come down and speak to us, if he had a moment.

Mr Whitbread apparently did have a moment, because not long after we saw him coming down the staircase. He was a white, middle-aged man with not very much hair, and though we all gave him cheery smiles when we made eye contact, I could have sworn I saw him roll his eyes. He gestured for us to come over to the foot of the staircase, so we thanked the woman at the desk and walked over to him, where it was less crowded. I expected us to be asked upstairs to his office, but instead he planted his shiny shoes firmly at the bottom of the staircase and put his hands in the pockets of his suit jacket.

'You're wanting a flag flown, are you?' he said, instead of *hello*. 'What's it for?' He held a hand out, palm up, like he was waiting to be handed something. Did he want us to hand the flag over? Or was he expecting a letter?

Daisy decided that what he really wanted was a handshake, and took hold of his hand. 'Nice to meet you,' she said, in the falsely cheerful voice her mum uses when talking to me. 'I'm Daisy Adewumi, and this is Ash Choudhary and Jamie Rambeau. We'd really love it if you could fly a flag for Non-Binary Day.'

'It's in July,' I added, as Mr Whitbread extracted his hand.

He frowned, and looked at us one by one. 'Some sort of Pride flag, is it?' he asked eventually. 'We already fly a flag for Pride Month. And for the parade. And for Transgender Day of Remembrance.' He sighed, as if flying these flags was causing him emotional strain. 'Do we really need another one?'

'Well, not many people seem to know what being non-binary is,' I said, feeling nervous again. 'So I'd like to raise some awareness. More people should be thinking about it, right? And you see, on a personal note, there's split-up schools in this area – one for boys and one for girls, so where does that leave non-binary kids like me? The flag could start a lot of conversations about non-binary rights.'

Mr Whitbread pinched between his eyes in the universal gesture for being fed up with listening. 'I'm sorry, is this some made-up transgender rights thing?' he asked. 'I don't mind supporting Pride and the related causes, but I'm not about to start flying a flag for every random kid who turns up saying their gender is a penguin.'

I've heard this rubbish before. People will try to make being non-binary sound as weird as possible to avoid accepting it as a concept. And no matter how many idiots you hear saying that sort of thing, it stings every single time.

'Actually, it's not made up,' I said, my voice shaking.

'I'm sorry?' Mr Whitbread was frowning.

'It's not been made up at all, it's very old,' I explained. 'Loads of ancient and indigenous cultures don't have binary-gendered societies at all, it's only recently that it's become the way a lot of the Western world thinks. There are the Hijra in India, and those who are known as two-spirited people in Native American culture, the muxe in Mexico, and the bakla in the Philippines—'

'And in Britain?' Mr Whitbread asked, exasperated. 'Anything a bit closer to home?'

'There's loads of non-binary British people,' I said. 'I'm one of them.'

Daisy raised her chin. 'I think this conversation has proved that we need more awareness, don't you think?'

'It would be a good way to show support,' Ash added.

The three of us beamed at Mr Whitbread like eager kittens.

But his face stayed as bored as ever. 'I don't think so, no,' he said. 'Sorry. Flying a flag of support is serious, it's not a joke. You can't come in here with your imaginary genders and expect everyone to start flying your flag. What's next? People saying they're really cats or dogs?'

'I'm not an animal, or imaginary,' I snapped. 'I'm a person, and people should—'

'Should?' He smirked. 'Sounds a bit entitled, don't you think?'

I realised then. This wasn't important to Mr Whitbread, not at all. He wasn't losing anything by mocking me, or by telling me no. He hadn't even acknowledged the schools issue.

And that made my blood boil.

'Can you at least give it some thought?' Daisy was saying. 'Non-Binary Day isn't until July, so you could think about it, or ask people in the local area what they thought?'

'No.' Mr Whitbread yawned, covering his mouth with the back of his hand. 'No, I don't think so, kids. Sorry. Come back when you've got something real to go on.' Then without a goodbye, he turned and walked back up the steps.

I watched him go, feeling like my entire body was on fire. I barely noticed Daisy and Ash tugging my sleeves to pull me out of the building and back to the steps outside. They were talking over my head about what to do next as I sat down on the stone steps, trying to blink away the flashing black spots in my vision. All of a sudden, the annoyance and tiredness I'd been feeling over all this – choosing between the schools, choosing between Ash and Daisy, being treated like I was making all this up – those feelings seemed ready to explode out of me.

Making a fuss is sometimes what you have to do to get listened to. Olly's words came back to me. *What do you think Pride is all about?*

He was right. I'd spent so long trying to gently convince people of the most basic thing: that I should be allowed to exist. I was fed up with it. I wanted to do something loud, something big, and something no one would be able to ignore.

If I was Olly, I would have kicked and screamed and probably broken a window or two, but I was me. And I had a better idea.

I fished the huge striped flag back out of my backpack, and looked at it, feeling determined.

'Jamie?' Ash asked, looking worried.

'I'm going to get that flag up there,' I said, standing up. I felt super-charged, electric, on fire with my new idea. 'Right now. I'm going to get it onto that flagpole right now and no one is going to stop me.'

I turned and marched straight back into the building, Daisy and Ash hot on my heels.

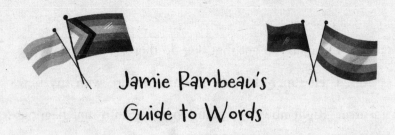

Jamie Rambeau's Guide to Words

Protest

A **protest** is a public expression of objection, disapproval or dissent against an idea or action, typically a political one. Protests can take many different forms, from individual statements to mass demonstrations. They could be a big march through a city, a single person standing holding a sign . . .

. . . or three kids climbing onto the roof of the Council House.

12

No one gave us a second glance as we went back in. No one stopped us as we went up the staircase, looking for signs for how to get to the roof.

I had expected Ash to be dribbling with fear, but I think he was being powered by anger as well, because he didn't look scared for once. Daisy however was glancing around nervously as we got to the top of the stairs. Ahead of us there was a locked door at the top landing that you needed a key-card to open. There was also an intercom button though, so I pressed it.

Beep.

'Hello?' It sounded like the lady at the desk downstairs. I didn't know if there was a camera watching me along with the mic, so I smiled cheerily just in case.

'Hi! We're just going through to Mr Whitbread's office!'

I'd got that from Olly, who used the same technique to get into the spa at the gym. You don't say *please can I go through*, you say *I am going through*, like it's already been planned and agreed, and people won't argue with you.

He was right.

'Right-o,' the voice said, and the door went *clunk* before opening a crack. We pushed it the rest of the way, and walked in. There was another reception desk ahead, but there was no one sitting behind it, and then there were doors coming off the circular bit of the room, all with labels on.

We couldn't linger. The lady on reception could call

Mr Whitbread to check we'd found him.

'How do we know which door?' Daisy muttered.

'We need to find more stairs,' I said. 'We're not high enough for the roof.'

'The fire escape,' Ash said quietly. 'That will go up to the roof. The only problem is, opening the fire escape door will probably set the fire alarm off as well.'

I shrugged. 'That's OK with me. Everyone will have to leave, giving us time to protest properly.' I took a deep breath. 'It'll cause a big fuss.'

Ash went a bit pale, but didn't argue as we looked up for the Fire Exit signs. There were plenty, all pointing to a single door. There were also some pointing back down the main stairs.

'We've got one shot at this,' I said. 'We need to open the door and shut it behind us and go straight up onto the roof, OK?'

My friends nodded, and for a second I felt so proud of

them and so happy to know them. We were going to do this! But, as we got to the door, I hesitated. My electric feeling faded a little bit, letting the nerves creep back in.

'What's wrong?' Daisy asked.

I looked at her. 'Do you think I'm being selfish?'

'What? No, of course you're not,' she said firmly. 'Why'd you think that?'

'Because . . . this doesn't affect you, or Ash.' I nodded at him. 'You two are both sorted for your schools, and no one gets your pronouns wrong, and you've got toilets designed and labelled just for you. This . . . is just my issue. I'm dragging you two into it.'

'Incorrect,' Daisy said. 'You're our best friend, and we love you, and we care about things that affect you. It matters to us. You shouldn't have to put up with this sort of stuff by yourself. It's rubbish. It's a great, big, steaming pile of horse manure, that's what it is. And I hate it. We might not be able to change it,' she said, as she put her hand to the fire escape door, 'but we can shout out to everyone that our best friend shouldn't be an afterthought or an optional extra. That non-binary people are part of the world same as me and Ash and everyone else.'

Ash put his hand on the door, too. 'She's right,' he said. 'We might not be listened to, but we can shout. We'll always shout for you, Jamie.'

I opened my mouth to speak, but no words came out.

'I've been thinking about that presentation afternoon,' Daisy said. 'Back when those teachers came in to do the meeting. You must have felt awful, sitting there with no one having thought about you.'

'I – I'm used to it,' I said, though my throat hurt. 'I always have to stick up for myself.'

Ash patted me on the arm. 'You shouldn't have to do it on your own. We'll do better. We can start right here.'

My eyes started to sting. I think that's what friendship

is, in the end – people who'll stick up for you when everyone's watching, not just in private.

We looked at each other. Then, together, we pushed the fire escape door open.

The alarm immediately started to scream.

*

The fire escape steps clearly hadn't been used for a while. The metal was rusty and creaky. There was a breeze-block to one side of the door that looked like it was supposed to be used to prop it open. We nipped through the door and slammed it shut behind us.

Then, the handle came off in Daisy's hand.

'Oops,' she said, staring at it. 'Now how are we going to get back down?'

'Let's worry about that later,' I said, starting up the iron staircase. In no time at all, we were on the roof.

It was super windy up there, blowing a gale it felt like. The rainbow flag we'd seen earlier was fluttering proudly

160

with the pull of the breeze. That made me feel a bit braver.

I unfolded my flag and tried to work out how to attach it to the ropes that hung from the third flagpole. The ropes were all knotted together and slapping against the pole going *ting ting ting*. Daisy dug the face paints out of her bag, and Ash peered nervously over the edge of the building.

We could still hear the fire alarm screaming from inside.

'They've all gone outside,' Ash observed. 'They must have evacuated downstairs, thought it was a fire drill. Or maybe they think it's a real fire.'

'You don't think the fire brigade will come, do you?' Daisy said suddenly.

'I hope not,' I said uneasily. 'There.' I finished tying the flag in place, and the three of us yanked on the ropes until the yellow, white, purple and black flag rose into the air and fluttered wonderfully, if a little bit squashed-ly thanks to my knots in the rope.

I looked up at the yellow, white, purple and black striped flag proudly, my heart rising up to the clouds with it. This was the first time I'd ever seen the non-binary flag flying. I hoped that if there was another non-binary person in town today, they would see it. Maybe it would be the first ever time they'd seen it flying too.

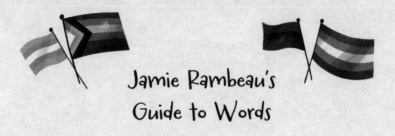

Jamie Rambeau's Guide to Words

Consequences

Definition: a result or effect, typically one that is unwelcome or unpleasant.

13

They figured out what we'd done after about ten minutes.

The problem was, even once they knew what had happened, they couldn't get us down from the roof. It turned out that without the handle, the fire escape door couldn't be opened at all, and now we were stuck up there.

Still, things could have been worse. We'd definitely got everyone's attention, and that felt hecking BRILLIANT.

Wearing the stripy face paint in non-binary colours,

that Daisy had painted onto our cheeks, the three of us leaned over the edge of the roof and waved and cheered at the growing crowd, which eventually began to attract what looked like news cameras and reporters. There was a helicopter circling overhead, and people kept cheering whenever one of us waved. It was fun! People were shouting at us, but in a nice way, and after a while I noticed that a few people in the crowd were waving rainbow flags and other flags with different colour stripes as well, and I felt like I could step right off the roof and fly.

I'd done it. I'd DONE IT! I'd caused a fuss, and people were actually *happy* about it. I wanted to scream with joy, to climb the flagpole and hang off the flag, to shout my name off the rooftop because I had made people look, and talk, and pay attention. It felt *fantastic*.

Not everyone was happy though.

'We're in so much trouble,' Ash whimpered as a news

reporter shouted up at us with a megaphone. He'd clearly reached his limit with rule-breaking and was now trapped in a worry-spiral.

'What . . . demands . . . have . . . ?' We heard the reporter bellowing through the megaphone, though he still sounded far away. 'Why . . . you . . . roof . . . ?' We couldn't hear him properly over the wind.

I pointed up at the flag, and waved my arm around a bit, and the crowd on the ground cheered again. I felt like a conductor in front of an orchestra. 'I can't believe we did this. Do you think they know it's the non-binary flag? I can see some people wearing rainbows down there.'

'Someone will know,' Daisy said calmly, looking over the edge of the roof. 'The helicopter on its own will make this huge news. We've pretty much seized control of the building, haven't we?'

Behind us were more bangs, shouting and swearing

noises as people tried and failed to get through the broken steel door.

We all looked at each other, and burst out laughing. This whole thing was bonkers, bananas, completely off the chain, but here we were actually doing it and people were *supporting* us! At that moment, I felt like I could handle any punishment that might arrive.

Just then, the fire brigade arrived.

'Oh, no,' Daisy said, watching the red engine pull in front of the building. The crowd of supporters parted to let it through, but to my surprise, they didn't move away completely. 'Oh no oh no oh no oh no we're in so much trouble now.'

'It's alright, firefighters are friends,' Ash said. But his expression changed when a police van pulled up next to it. 'Nope, cancel that. We're going down.'

At the sight of the police van, I think I blacked out for a minute. Sometimes your mind can do that to save itself from melting with panic. When I tuned back into reality my only thought was wondering how badly we were going to be punished. We were in deep poo, that was for sure. Our supporters were still there, though, which made me feel a tiny bit braver.

The firefighters started raising a cherry-picker lift off the back of the engine. It rose up slowlyyyyy like it was dragging things out to make us feel worse.

'Gentlepeople,' Daisy said solemnly, taking her hat off and holding it in front of her heart, 'it's been an honour protesting with you, tonight.'

Ash went pea-green as the lift got level with the roof, and an extremely large firefighter stepped off it. He had a harness clipping him on to the cage.

'Do you know what the penalty is for falsely setting off a fire alarm?' he thundered. With his helmet and goggles on, he looked terrifying and he sounded furious.

We shook our heads, too scared to speak.

'A year in prison,' he snarled. 'I hope you've got your bags packed.'

Ash didn't even squeak with fear. He straight-up fainted, folding on to the roof like an accordion. The rest of us stood staring at him.

'Huh.' The firefighter pushed his goggles up, and I saw he had a kind face despite his harsh tone. He sighed as he looked at us properly. 'Didn't mean to frighten the life out of the poor kid. Sorry. I thought you were a bit older than you actually are. I'll get this lad down first, then.' He stepped far enough on to the roof to scoop Ash up under the arms and get him into the cherry-picker cage. 'I'll be back for the two of you. Don't go anywhere.' He winked before pulling his goggles back down.

'Ha, ha,' we laughed weakly, watching the machine take Ash and the firefighter down and out of sight.

'Poor Ash,' I said, my heart sinking just like the cherry-picker.

'Poor us.' Daisy snorted. She paced a bit, the wind trying in vain to pull her hair out of her ponytail. 'I didn't think it would get this serious. Do you think we'll end up in court?'

'I don't think so . . . we're not eighteen. But I bet we get a caution.' I knew about cautions because Olly had two of them, one for throwing eggs at a police car during a student strike, and another for riding his bike down what he thought what a disused railway line (spoiler: it was very much *not* disused). I was trying to reassure Daisy, but the truth was, I was terrified. It was a good job I'd already been to the toilet because if not, this would definitely have been a spare underpants situation. My legs were shaking and my stomach seemed to have been replaced with a big bowl of blancmange. I'd never been in trouble – not *real* trouble – before. This felt like jumping off the 10m diving board when you can't even swim.

The firefighter came back for Daisy next, who waved

goodbye to me sadly as she dropped down out of sight. For a few minutes, I was on my own on top of the roof.

The wind blew hard, ruffling my coat as I looked up at the flag I'd raised. I took some photos of it flying, to keep on my phone forever. Looking at the flag again, the horrible churning feeling inside me lessened, just a little bit. I still felt horrible, but I felt proud of what I'd done as well. Even if I got into trouble, it had been worth it to have my flag flying over the city. I had pride.

It was my turn in the cherry-picker next.

'Watch your step,' the firefighter said. He clipped a mucky harness around my middle. 'Now, try not to throw up. I hate it when people throw up in here.'

I was about to say I almost never throw up when we started going down rather suddenly and my stomach did consider making a quick exit via my mouth. But after the initial jolt, we dropped back down the rest of the way slowly and steadily, the arm of the cherry-picker folding up neatly into the fire engine. As I came into sight, the crowd on the ground cheered, and I gave them a little wave before the firefighter told me to keep my arms in the cage.

'What did you have to go and do all that for, anyway?' he asked, nodding up at the roof. 'You realise you're going straight to the police station?'

I swallowed. 'It was a protest,' I said.

'So I've heard.' He looked at the flags I had painted onto my cheeks, and said more gently, 'It must mean a lot to you.'

I nodded. 'Everything.'

He nodded. 'Next time, keep your protests on ground level, please.'

We reached the ground and he unclipped me and let me out of the cage. 'Watch your step. They want you to go straight over to the—'

But he hadn't even finished speaking when I

173

was immediately surrounded by microphones and cameras and people wearing rainbow flags wrapped around their shoulders.

'Over here! Why were you up on the roof!' someone yelled.

'Why did you take over the building?' someone else shouted.

'Do you have something to say to the leader of the local council?' a third reporter asked.

'It was a protest,' I said, trying not to screw my face up as cameras flashed. I had no idea where to look, there were too many lenses and faces and foamy microphones that were so huge they looked like loaves of black bread on sticks. 'We were protesting and raising awareness.'

'What for? What were you raising awareness of?'

I thought this was a stupid question – hadn't they seen the flag? But then I realised that this was the whole point of everything we'd done. Not everyone would know what the flag meant, not everyone even knew non-binary kids like me existed. By putting it up, we'd got people interested, asking questions, wanting to know more. A spark of bravery flared in my chest. This was my only chance to make a fuss and get heard and I had to use it wisely. 'We were protesting to raise awareness of non-binary rights,' I said. 'Did you know that for secondary school, kids in this area have to choose between a boys' school or a girls'?'

There was an undercurrent of surprised muttering. 'Well, they do,' I said loudly. 'And I'm not a boy or a girl. I'm non-binary and I want to . . . I want to . . .'

'Yes?' The reporter's face was excited. 'What is it you want?'

'I want to stay with my friends,' I blurted out. 'But I can't because we're all going to be split up, girls going to the girls' school, boys to the boys' and people like me left stuck. Whoever I choose to be with, I've got to pretend

I'm something I'm not. I'm a non-binary kid and I shouldn't have to change or lie about who I am!'

There was a massive cheer from our rainbow-wearing supporters, and I gave the biggest grin of my life. They could have clamped handcuffs on me right at that moment and I don't think I would have even noticed. I was floating on a cloud of my own daring.

'And there we have it!' The reporter turned back to yell at his news camera as a police officer put a hand on my shoulder and started to steer me towards the van. 'An inspiring statement there from one of the young protestors, about an issue that is clearly important to . . . I'm sorry, what's your name?' he shouted.

'I'm Jamie! Jamie Rambeau!' I shouted back through the crowd.

'That's an impassioned speech there,' the reporter shouted into his camera, 'from local resident, Jamie Rainbow!'

And as the police van doors slammed shut on my view, I wasn't even mad about the new name he'd given me.

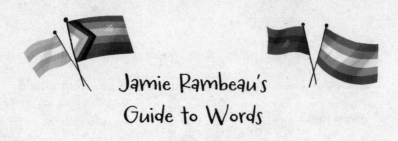

Jamie Rambeau's
Guide to Words

Manifesto

Your **manifesto** is a list of things you want to make happen, or things you want to change. We sort of wrote one when we made our list of demands back at Ash's house. When I told the reporter, 'I want to stay with my friends', that was a sort of manifesto too.

Things on a manifesto could be short-term goals, like changing a name of a school, or long-term massive goals, like getting a law passed.

14

We didn't actually get arrested.

Turns out, real life isn't like the films – at least it wasn't for us. I kept expecting someone to tell me I had the right to remain silent or to shine a big lightbulb into my face, but we just rode away in silence. I was in the back of the van with Daisy and Ash and two other officers, who alternated between looking disapproving and giving each other slightly amused looks. I worried that they were thinking up dire and hilarious punishments for us, possibly involving piranhas or long stretches in prison with only bread and water.

The tension and the silence built up to oppressive levels, and I was on edge waiting for the axe to fall, but when we got to the station we were just told to sit and wait for our parents. We were even given biscuits and squash and blankets because we were all cold from being on the roof for so long. They sat us in a bit of the waiting room around the corner from the entrance, where it was a bit more private but we could still see the automatic front doors sliding open now and again as people came and went. The officers at the desk were keeping an eye on us without hovering too closely.

The silence in the station was super weird and highly suspicious. I wondered why they weren't at least telling us off – until our parents arrived and I realised that the police being nice to us was all a *strategy*. I've seen this sort of thing on police shows. They do this performance called 'Good Cop, Bad Cop', where one of them is nice to you and the other one is mean, to try and get you to talk. Well, the police had all bet on our parents falling automatically into the role of Bad Cop, so they'd given us the kind treatment to soften us up.

They were right to bank on Parental Bad Cops.

I have never, in all my life, seen my dad so angry. Not when Olly pierced his own eyebrow in the bathroom, or when the people at the garage accidentally set the car upholstery on fire. Not even the time the trick-or-treaters toilet-papered the front of the house and it rained so hard the paper got fused on to the brickwork. This was a whole new level of rage. He was so angry he couldn't speak, like his teeth had been welded together with fury. He just made noises in the back of his throat at the officer who explained why I was there, then took a seat next to me without looking at me once, his whole body vibrating like the anger was a swarm of bees trapped under his skin.

I didn't dare say a word. There was nothing I could

say to make this better and I was worried that even breathing too loudly might be the spark that made my dad actually explode.

But, even though I'd turned my dad into Mount Vesuvius just waiting to blow, I still felt like I'd done the right thing. We'd got the flag flown and my message out into the world. We'd even been on TV. As far as raising awareness went, we'd done better than we'd thought we would. It was just a shame *how* it'd had to happen. I'd never liked breaking the rules, I'd always been a kid who did as I was told, but it seemed like sometimes the rules had to be broken if you wanted to be heard.

That didn't change the fact that we were up to our eyeballs in trouble. Ash was hiding deep inside his hoody to avoid the hissed stream of menace coming from his mother. Daisy and her mum had been taken into a small room to be interviewed. Denise was so ashamed of Daisy that she was covering her eyes.

I sat up straighter. I felt proud of my friends. They'd stuck by me and helped me do something incredibly brave and incredibly stupid, because they were my mates. Because they wanted to help *me*.

Suddenly, the thought of being separated from either of them smashed into my stomach like a football kicked at high speed, and I hunched over to try and make the pain go away. Jamie, Daisy and Ash. That's who we were, that's who we should always be. That's what was being torn apart, and it was me in the middle being ripped in half whichever way I went. It wasn't even the choosing I hated. It was the losing. Losing Daisy, or Ash, and a bit of myself, either way. I sat back, suddenly miserable. I remembered Mum saying something one day when she was going to a funeral of a friend's mother. She said that, at some point in life, you go to more funerals than weddings, and you lose more people than there are new babies. No one was dying in my situation, but it hurt that

I'd already reached the point where I was having things taken away.

Daisy and her mum were still in the interview room. Whilst the rest of us waited, we were given forms to fill in with our details. As usual, there was an M box and an F box on it to tick. In the past, I had ticked one of the boxes and moved on as fast as I could to get away from it. But I wasn't going to do that, not anymore. I'd had enough. *More* than enough. This was the police, not the doctor, and there was no reason I should have to tick either of the boxes.

Before, I would have ignored it.

Not anymore.

I got up quickly, and went over to the desk ready to educate someone, my arms and legs fizzing with nerves. But this was the new me – I wasn't going to be polite and passive, I was going to point out when things were wrong. Because if I didn't, no one else would.

'Excuse me,' I said to the officer behind the desk. 'I can't fill this in.'

The officer at the desk looked up at me. 'Why not?'

'Because there's only "M" or "F" options on it,' I said, as patiently as I could manage. 'And I'm not "M" or "F", so what should—'

'JAMIE, FOR GOD'S SAKE!'

Dad had finally exploded. He came up behind me, invisible angry lava spilling out of him, so hot you could almost feel it. He marched over and snatched the form, creasing it badly down the middle. 'Will you just PICK ONE and stop it with this? You're not special, you're the same as everyone else. Stop attention-seeking. Just tick a damned box, will you? Stop making everything all about you.'

I stared at him, eyes wide. For the first time in my life I was slightly afraid of my dad. I've never been scared of him before, not once. But right then, I was. I wasn't scared that he was going to hit me or anything like that, I know for certain he never would. What I was afraid of was the words he was saying. *Pick one*. He wanted me to pick one. Maybe he wouldn't love me unless I did. That's what I was afraid of.

Even though I was shaking all over, I made myself shake my head once more. No. No, I wouldn't pick one. Not now, and not ever.

He wasn't even looking.

He took the paper back to his seat and started filling it in for me. I didn't even know which box he'd ticked for me – whether he'd chosen to have a daughter or a son – and I didn't want to know. It was clear to me now: I was never going to be what he wanted.

I wanted to cry, but I refused to, screwing my face and hands up so tight something inside me went *creak*.

Daisy and her mum came out of the interview room then. Denise's expression had softened a tiny bit, but she still had her nose in the air and refused to look at me as they walked out of the building. When they were gone, I relaxed, just a fraction. It looked like I'd never be asked over to the Adewumi house again as long as I lived, but it wasn't as though that was the end of the world. Besides, if Daisy had been allowed to leave, it didn't seem like we'd be going to jail.

Unless they were saving that for me, the ring-leader and criminal mastermind of the whole scheme.

I was left wondering about my fate a bit longer, because Ash and Sana were called in next. I had no choice but to sit down next to my dad again, who had finished the paperwork and was now sending texts and muttering under his breath.

I watched him for a minute before speaking. 'I'm sorry,' I tried.

He pocketed his phone. 'What for?'

A trick question if ever there was one. 'I'm sorry

for . . .' I floundered.

Dad took a deep breath, the sort adults take when they're about to use the sing-song voice of *I'm Not Angry, I'm Disappointed*. Except that didn't happen. He didn't say anything at all, actually. He just heaved out the breath like it was some heavy burden he was letting go of. Maybe the burden was me.

I blinked, taken aback. This was a new kind of reaction. Eleven years of predictable parent behaviour and it had been replaced by something I didn't know how to deal with. I wondered if I should apologise again, if that was the key to cracking this strange new code.

But then, he spoke. And he sounded extremely tired. 'I don't understand,' he said. 'That's becoming more obvious by the day. I want to understand you, Jamie, but I don't.'

My mouth opened to say that that wasn't *my* fault, but I stopped.

'I didn't think this was that big of a deal,' he said softly. 'I genuinely didn't think it was the sort of thing you'd get yourself into trouble over, I just thought it was . . . a way of defining yourself.'

'It is,' I said. 'It defines me and it *is* me. It's not a badge I can take on and off. It's me twenty-four hours a day, seven days a week. I have to think about that part of myself *all the time*.'

'All the time?' He looked at me, eyebrows furrowed.

'All the time,' I repeated. 'Like with that form. And toilets. And schools. And clothes shops and other shops and the doctors and everything.' I slumped down in my seat. 'I wanted it to not be a big deal. So I didn't say anything when people got it wrong or when there were only two options on a questionnaire. Because I didn't want to make a fuss.'

Dad's eyes had gone wide.

'But no one else has made a fuss for me,' I carried on,

my voice starting to crack. 'And – and when we went to that meeting at school and I realised no one had thought *What about Jamie*, I . . .' I stopped, because the cracking in my throat had turned into sharp shards that were stuck painfully in my neck, making it painful to speak.

My dad put his hand over mine, and it was warm and comforting and I almost felt like I was six or seven again and I'd come to him for a love after falling off my bike or something. 'I didn't mean to shout at you,' he said. 'I'm sorry for that, I really am. It scares me. Seeing you put yourself out there like that and have people looking funny at you. That's not what I wanted for your life. I want you to be able to be who you are without anyone caring.'

Some of the shards in my neck that had been stopping me from speaking melted a little and I realised I'd been wrong to be scared before. My dad loved me. He was just scared, too. About me having to be loud all the time.

About how other people thought of me. Maybe how they thought of him, too.

I turned my hand around and squeezed his. 'I used to feel like that,' I said. 'Like . . . it would be better to be quiet. Safer. But I don't want to be quiet, not anymore.'

'Jamie Rambeau?' a police officer called.

I looked up and saw Ash and his mother just leaving the building. It was my turn, then. I swallowed hard, dislodging some more of the sharp spikes in my throat, and stood. I had no idea what was going to happen now.

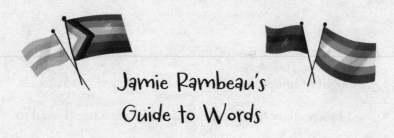

Jamie Rambeau's
Guide to Words

Stereotypes

Stereotypes are limiting and untrue ideas about people, or groups, or things. These stereotypical ideas are often assumed to be the facts, even if they're not. Stereotypes, even if they're said with good intentions, can really be negative and hurtful.

A stereotype could be something fairly harmless, like thinking all English people wear bowler hats and carry umbrellas. Or it could be hurtful, like thinking that you can only be non-binary if you look androgynous. Neither of these things are true!

15

The interview room was warm. Unpleasantly so, like sitting in an oven. I wondered if it was deliberate. There were two police officers sitting at the table, a man and a woman, and though they both looked tired, the woman smiled as me and my dad sat down.

'You're not under arrest,' she said to me as soon as we were seated. Her clipped-on ID said *Police Constable Saidu*. 'So you don't have to answer any questions if you don't want to. The council isn't going to press charges.'

The man, a Sergeant Moran, addressed my dad.

'After the demonstration of support on the ground, they felt it would be a bad PR move to prosecute the kids.'

'Why am I here then?' I asked.

'We want to ask you what happened,' Constable Saidu said. 'Would you be able to tell us?'

I stayed silent, not knowing where to begin.

Sergeant Moran's gaze moved from my dad to me. 'You friends told me you were doing a protest. Did you plan to do it on the roof?'

'I didn't plan to do a protest at all,' I said, trying not to squirm on the slippery plastic seat. 'It just sort of happened. We went there to ask the council to fly my flag but Mr Whitbread said he wouldn't. He said my gender was made-up and I was wasting his time.' I folded my arms. 'If he'd listened to what I had to say, I wouldn't have gone up there.'

Both of the officers nodded, checking through some papers which presumably contained Ash's and Daisy's stories. 'That's what your friends have told us, yes,' Sergeant Moran said. 'You do realise you wasted considerable time and money of the police and the fire service?'

'We didn't mean to get stuck,' I said. 'That bit was an accident. Sorry.'

The officer pinched between his eyes. 'Look, kid,' he said. 'I get protesting for your rights, I really do. My husband and I go to Pride every year, we know the history. But there are better ways of doing it, OK? Next time, no rooftop shenanigans, got it?'

'Got it,' I said, because it wouldn't have been wise to say anything else.

There were a few more forms to sign after that, but it looked as though I'd well and truly gotten away with it. Not even a caution! Olly would find that hilarious, I thought.

We collected my belongings from the front desk, which were my flag and backpack, and finally left the station as it was starting to get dark. Dad kept a hand on my arm as we walked out, as if he was worried I'd disappear if he let go of me. I didn't mind.

When we got to the car park, I noticed a person leaning against the wall of the building, playing on their phone. They looked up sharply when we went past, then staggered upright. 'Hey – Jamie Rainbow, isn't it?'

'Rambeau. And no, thank you,' Dad said firmly as if he was declining a copy of *The Big Issue*. 'We just want to go home.'

'I'm not a reporter or anything,' the person said, holding their hands up, one of them still full of phone. 'Wait, here.' They fished a business card out of their pocket and held it out. It was soft and furry around the edges, but there was a rainbow on it. Dad held it for me to read. It said:

Stevie Zhang, **PRIDE SOC.** President

'What's a Pride soc?' I asked, thinking about stripey footwear.

'It's short for Society.' Stevie smiled. They had short, black spikey hair and a lot of pins of their jacket, same as me. I noticed that one of them said *They/Them/Theirs* and my stomach jolted a bit in delight. 'I'm the president of the LGBTQ society at the university. It was us who were on the ground waving the flags.'

'Oh!' I grinned. 'Thanks. That was awesome of you. Apparently all the support meant the council didn't press charges.'

'Really? That's great. Well, I just wanted to make sure they let you out and everything.' They nodded at the police station. 'And also to say . . . if you ever want to have a chat about anything . . . fundraising or protests and awareness-raising or a whinge about the genders, my details are on the card.' They looked at Dad. 'You too, sir. I'm always on the end of an email, even if you're not a student.'

'Thanks,' I said, putting the card in my pocket. 'But I don't have any more protests planned. I think I'd better keep my head down for a bit.'

'Why?' Stevie asked, sounding genuinely baffled. 'You've pulled off a rooftop protest to raise awareness, haven't you? You've got to build on that! Heck, I didn't know the schools here were separated like that until you said so. I bet loads of people don't know, or never thought about it because it's always been that way. You've made it into something people can't ignore anymore!'

My stomach rolled even harder at that, but this time there were sparks of excitement in it, too. 'OK, but . . . what do I do next? The schools aren't going to change just because I made a fuss, are they?'

Stevie waggled a finger. 'Never say never, Jamie. Someone's got to be the one to change the world. It might as well be you.'

*

Dad invited Stevie back home with us for tea. He usually distrusts anyone he meets randomly, but after checking their credentials on the rather impressive university website, he relaxed and started chatting away to Stevie about the ice hockey team they both supported. They were the sort of person you couldn't help liking.

When we pulled on to the drive at home, we were met by the sight of Olly, who was wearing a non-binary flag (I have no idea where he got it from) as a cape, and flying around the front garden like he was a little kid pretending to be Superman.

'You total legend!' he screamed as I got out. He picked me up and spun me around before dropping me. 'My little sibling caused city-wide chaos!' He turned to the street, which was empty – though there were plenty of people peeping through their blinds and curtains – and bellowed, 'Your sibling could never!'

Dad ignored him and went to the front door whilst Stevie stood looking amused on the driveway. 'Nice to see you've got support at home,' they said.

Olly paused in his shouting to do a comic double-take at the visitor. 'Hey,' he said, suddenly dropping his screaming act and coming over. 'I'm Olly.'

'Stevie,' they said, and the two of them shook hands. 'So, you're Jamie's brother?'

'Yes,' Olly beamed with his lipsticked mouth. 'Are you here because of the rooftop thing?'

'Yeah. I'm with the university.'

I followed them both inside and into the sitting room. Stevie was telling Olly all about their role and Olly was listening in silence. That was unusual. Olly liked to lead conversations, not be led within them.

When we were all perched on armchairs and sofas, Mum walked in. She opened her mouth angrily but Dad jumped up and took her into the hallway. I could hear them speaking quietly and when she came back in the fight was gone from her face.

'I'm so glad you're safe, Jamie,' she said. 'Now, why don't I make us all some hot chocolate, and you can tell us what's going on?'

'I don't want to start acting like some sort of campaign manager,' Stevie said after we all had mugs in hand, 'but Jamie's cause is obviously one that's close to my own heart. My school was mixed, but I still had split PE and things like that, which made life uncomfortable.'

'Maybe a campaign manager would be helpful,' I said, thinking about me and my friends' campaigns so far, none of which had exactly gone to plan – although the last one had certainly been attention-grabbing. 'I've shouted and screamed, but I don't know if that's going to change anything.' My stomach squirmed at the thought of Mrs Bailey or Mr Dean watching the news and seeing me and my friends. Would they be impressed or horrified?

Stevie pulled a thoughtful face. 'If you could wish for any outcome, what would you wish for?' they asked.

I went red. 'If I could wish for anything, I'd wish that me and Ash and Daisy could all go to the same school.'

Stevie smiled sadly. 'I understand. But that might not be possible. The two schools are probably not going to entirely change before September. But if we have to live with there being two different schools, is there anything that would make it better for you?'

This was harder, but I decided to be honest. 'If they dropped the "for boys" and "for girls" from the school names,' I said thoughtfully, 'and didn't have the rules about how you have to identify, then . . . I'd be happy with that, I think.'

'So, it's the label that's the crux of the problem.' Stevie nodded, tapping their chin. 'Alright, that gives us something solid to work with.'

Mum frowned. 'You really think you can get a school

to change their name and intake?'

'I don't see why not.' Stevie shrugged. 'Ideally, both of them would. But even one would be a victory.'

'But everyone around here would still know it was the school for boys or girls, because they know the history,' I pointed out.

'Well, we could ask them to make a statement as well. On their social media, or somewhere else public,' Stevie explained patiently. 'Ask them to announce that they will be accommodating pupils of any gender, and prove they've got the facilities to do so. The old-fashioned newspaper press would pick it up after that.'

I sighed. 'They won't do that. Mrs Bailey and Mr Dean, neither of them seemed like they wanted to try.'

'Maybe they won't, but I think it's worth a go.' Stevie stood up, and stretched. 'Changing the world is hard work. We've been at it for decades, centuries even. Sometimes it feels like you're up against a brick wall but if you get enough people behind you, even walls can be knocked down. We're not going anywhere, and people can't expect us to be quiet. Change can be small and slow, like getting one school to change their admissions policy, or it can be big like getting a new law passed nationwide. Neither is less important than the other. Lots of little changes snowball together into one big change, after all.'

I found I was smiling. Olly was looking at Stevie like they were sparkling. 'OK,' I said. 'OK, let's . . . let's do it.'

Stevie grinned. 'Brilliant. Let's let the dust settle for a day or two, see how the news decides to spin the footage of your protest. And then we'll make a plan.'

*

It was super embarrassing watching myself on the local news. It had already played by the time Stevie left to catch the bus home, but Olly brought it up on the iPlayer and we all sat watching as the story was shown in high-definition.

The segment opened with a shot of the Council House and the busy marketplace down below.

'This afternoon, the city centre was brought to a standstill after three young protestors took over the roof of the Nottingham Council House,' the report began. 'What began as a high-spirited attempt to fly a Pride flag over the city soon turned into chaos as the protestors found themselves trapped on the roof.'

The picture changed to show a drone-shot of me, Ash and Daisy on the roof, waving and pointing at the non-binary flag, which got a decent amount of screen time, I was pleased to note.

Olly ruffled my hair. 'You're famous, look at you!'

'Shh,' Mum hissed.

'The three protestors were later rescued by the emergency services . . .' The footage now showed the three of us being taken down in the cherry-picker thing with the firefighter. Ash had apparently stayed unconscious until he got to the ground. When it was my turn they got my waving on camera, and then cut to the crowd of rainbow supporters who'd come to cheer us on.

'The protest attracted an outpouring of support from the city's LGBTQ community,' said the voiceover, 'as the raising of the non-binary flag was intended to promote awareness. The organiser of the protest, Jamie Rainbow, spoke to our reporter . . .'

'Jamie *What*?' Mum gasped as Olly hooted with laughter and almost fell off the sofa.

The little-me on TV, with black, purple, yellow and white stripes on their cheeks, was speaking, or rather squeaking, as the image cut between my face and the flag and back again: 'We were protesting to raise awareness of non-binary rights,' my squeaky voice said. 'Did you know that for secondary school, kids in this area have to choose between a boys' school or a girls'? Well, they do. And I'm not a boy or a girl. I'm non-binary, and I want to . . . I want to stay with my friends!'

The video cut to text on the screen:

Non-binary is an umbrella term for people whose gender identity doesn't sit comfortably with 'man' or 'woman'. Non-binary identities are varied and can include people who identify with some aspects of binary identities, while others reject them entirely.

Non-binary people can feel that their gender identity and gender experience involves being both a man and a woman, or that it is fluid, in between, or completely outside of that binary.

STONEWALL*

* https://www.stonewall.org.uk/about-us/news/10-ways-step-ally-non-binary-people

Then the segment cut back to me. 'But we're all going to be split up,' TV-me was saying, 'girls going to the girls' school, boys to the boys' and people like me left stuck. Whoever I choose to be with, I've got to pretend I'm something I'm not. I'm a non-binary kid and I shouldn't have to change or lie about who I am!' The cheering of the crowd seemed even louder coming through the TV and the news item finished with a note that the two schools in the area had declined to comment.

Olly switched it off. 'That,' he said, holding his hands up in surrender, 'was amazing. Literally the best thing I've ever seen, and I look at my own face twenty times a day. I mean, wow. You said it all.'

Dad was nodding. 'They did you proud there, including the information and everything. I was worried they were going to make you look ridiculous.' He put an arm around my shoulders and gave me a brief sideways hug. 'Proud of you, kid.'

I heaved out a breath as Dad let go of me. Mum got up and gave my arm a squeeze before going into the kitchen. That was high praise, coming from her. She was probably still angry, and definitely still disappointed, but she had softened. We'd be alright, I was sure of it.

Something had changed.

Olly squeezed beside me on the armchair, though there wasn't really room, and put his arm around me. 'I know everyone keeps saying it, but I'm so proud of you,' he said quietly.

I plucked at the non-binary flag he was still wearing like a cape. 'Where did you even get this?'

He shrugged. 'Bought it ages ago. When you first told me. I figured we might need it, one day.'

Suddenly my throat was feeling all tight and weird. Not like I was about to cry. At least, not like I was about to cry from being sad. I was the exact opposite of being sad. I was the least sad anyone had ever been right at that moment.

Olly pretended not to notice my sappy face. 'So.' He checked his nails. 'When are we seeing Stevie again?'

'Urgh.' I pushed him off the armchair. 'You *like* them?'

'What's not to like?' He grinned wickedly from the floor.

'I thought you liked boys,' I pointed out.

His grin widened. 'Guess I'm learning something about myself today. Labels aren't permanent, you know. You can change them any time you like.'

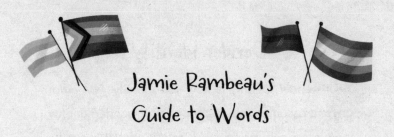

Jamie Rambeau's
Guide to Words

Gender

This is something that people often talk about in terms of 'masculinity' or 'femininity', as though they are two separate things. Gender is something that depends on the culture you are a part of, which can vary all over the world, but is usually assumed from whether doctors thought you were a boy or a girl when you were born. However, you cannot ever truly guess someone's gender.

Gender Expression

This is the way we present ourselves, which can include your physical appearance, your clothing, hairstyles and even how you behave. Remember, there's no wrong way to express yourself and your gender, as long as you're not hurting anyone else.

Gender Identity

Your gender identity is how you identify. Not what anyone assumes you might be. Your gender identity is your true self, inside you. **Gender identity** can be really important to who you are as a person, or just a small part of who you are. Whether you're a boy, a girl, agender, bigender, non-binary, genderfluid or anything else at all. Each person's experience with their gender identity is unique and personal.

16

We were celebrities at school on Monday. Well, maybe Notorious Villains was a better way of describing us. If swearing at that head teacher had got me a reputation, it was nothing compared to this. People wouldn't leave me, Ash or Daisy alone. Wanted to know if we'd been arrested, what prison was like, what had *really* happened on the roof, when was our next protest, and could they come and help out?

It was . . . kind of amazing. People weren't just talking to me, they were talking to Ash and Daisy as well, and they were listening to what we had to tell them! Even the teachers managed to sidle over for a chat at break or lunch and by the end of the first day we'd talked to practically everyone in the whole school. Miss Palanska managed to find excuses to give all three of us five merit marks in a single day (Ash got one for sharpening a pencil), and one of the dinner supervisors gave us all an extra scoop of ice cream to go with our butterscotch tart.

I was floating. I hadn't realised how many people would care and be happy about what had happened.

'Look at this,' Ash said after school, coming out of the corner shop where we usually bought reheated sausage rolls to eat on the way home. He wasn't holding a sausage roll today, he was holding the local newspaper. And guess who was on the front page.

'OH MY DAYS.' Daisy grabbed the paper and held it up like it was a sacred relic. 'Front page, Jamie! Front! Actual! Page!'

I couldn't speak. It felt like my stomach had fallen out of my bum.

'Local Kids Protest for LGBTQ Rights,' Daisy read the headline. 'Wow.' She opened the paper, turning to where the story continued.

'Are you alright?' Ash asked me, his nostrils flaring in concern.

'I don't know,' I said. 'I think so.'

Daisy flapped at us to be quiet. 'Listen! ". . . Mr Dean, Head of local school St Joseph's, was approached for comment, and said: 'We all greatly admire Jamie and their friends' bravery and determination, however we cannot condone or support rule-breaking'" . . . Ha. "The Head of Queen Elizabeth's declined to comment."'

'Shocking,' I said, sarcasm dripping onto the pavement. I took the paper. The photo on the front was a grainy shot of the Council House with the flag flying above it and the three of us looking like blobs alongside.

All the colours of the flag had bled into one another so that it looked a sort of dark grey. I tucked the paper under my arm to take it home with me anyway. Ash bought another copy to show his parents, but Daisy said her mum was pretending it never happened, so it was best if she went home empty-handed.

After saying bye to my friends at their houses, I was only mildly surprised to see Stevie talking to Olly in the front garden when I got to mine. There was a car I didn't recognise on the driveway, which I assumed belonged to Stevie. When they saw me, they gave a big wave. Olly looked mildly annoyed that I'd turned up.

'Have you even left the house today?' I asked him by way of a hello.

He pretended to gasp in deep offence, hand on his chest. 'I've been to college, I'll have you know.'

'Hm.' I narrowed my eyes at him. 'All day?'

'Enough of the day,' he said with a smirk.

Stevie pressed their mouth into a line to hide a laugh. 'Hey, Jamie. Good day?'

'We made the front page.' I passed them the paper. They opened it and Olly craned to see. 'It's not a great photo. But they did ask the head teachers of the schools to comment.'

'And?' Stevie looked up.

'One said they thought we were brave but we shouldn't break rules, and the other one didn't say anything at all.'

'Interesting.' Stevie rubbed their chin. 'Well, it's a start! Soon other people will chime in, too.'

'I guess. But it's only local news,' I said. 'It's not exactly getting the message far and wide, is it?'

Stevie grinned. 'Never underestimate the value of social media, Jamie.' They took out their phone, and opened Twitter, showing me the local news account, where the newspaper front page article had been posted. Then, they showed me the number of shares it had had.

It was in the *thousands*.

'How's it got that many?' I gasped, grabbing their phone.

'We shared it on the Pride Soc account.' Stevie laughed. 'With some supportive commentary of course. Everyone is talking about it.' They took their phone back, and showed me some of the comments.

> Justice for Jamie! Inspirational! – @LGBTQuarrior

> What's the point in separate schools for boys and girls? I don't get it??? – @TeacherOnTheTwitter87

> Such an old-fashioned idea, and not inclusive at all! – @SuperCat4Ever

> Students should go to the school best for them, not one based on what toilets they use! – @ParentsForPride2023

There were a few nasty comments as well, but Stevie scrolled past them quickly so I couldn't see. Most of them were positive – which should have been a good thing, but all of a sudden I wanted to vault over the low garden fence and leg it down the road and disappear. We were everywhere. We'd made a fuss, a real fuss, and now the whole world was going to know about it.

'I feel a bit sick,' I said.

Olly caught me around the shoulders. 'It's OK, Jamie, come and sit down.' He steered me to the front step and plonked me down onto it. 'It's a big deal, I know.'

I nodded. This *was* a big deal. The world was watching. Or at least, a small part of it. What did that mean for anyone else who was non-binary or queer and watching all this happen? Was I inspirational or was I making a giant mess of things? I had never meant to become a spokesperson for anything. I'd just wanted to go to secondary like my friends, on my own terms.

In an ideal world, being non-binary would be as ordinary and regular as having to wear glasses – something a lot of people do, but no one much cares about. But the fact was . . . it wasn't. It was still something people didn't consider. And until it was, I would have to keep battling away.

How long would that take? Years? Decades?

I suddenly felt exhausted.

As if reading my mind, Stevie came and sat down next to me. 'I get it,' they said. 'When you start thinking about everything that needs to change, it's too much. It's like looking directly at the sun – you shouldn't do it. But you're not doing this on your own, Jamie, OK? We've been doing this for a long time, me and my friends and their friends and all the way back through history. Changes can be fast or slow, they're unpredictable. But they do come. You don't have to change the world, but if we can get you into a school that won't make you call yourself a boy or a girl to get through the door, that's a good change. That's a small change that'll become part of a big one. Eventually.'

'What if I mess it all up?' I asked.

Stevie laughed. 'You won't. I promise. There's nothing wrong with wanting to be treated equally. For wanting people to accept you exist. This stuff on social media . . . it just proves that you're not alone. That there are people outside this little town who are rooting for you and want you to succeed. We cheered for you on the ground during your protest and we'll be cheering you on as long as you want us to. Because if you win, everyone wins. And then we'll all be celebrating.'

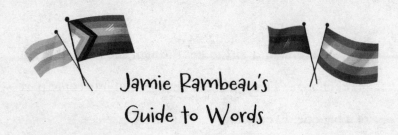

Jamie Rambeau's
Guide to Words

Flags

Lots of LGBTQ identities have their own flag. There are flags in every colour of the rainbow (plus an actual rainbow!). The non-binary flag is made up of yellow, white, purple and black stripes.

The non-binary pride flag was created in 2014 by Kye Rowan, and the four colours all have their own special meaning.

The yellow stripe represents people who would say their gender is somewhere outside of the binary of men and women; the purple stripe represents people whose gender identity is a mixture of (or somewhere in between) male and female; then the black stripe is to represent people who would say they have no gender; and finally the white stripe represents people who embrace many different genders – perhaps even all of them!

17

Our celebrity status at school didn't decline over the next few weeks. If anything, it ramped up. We got asked so many times about when our next protest was that Daisy started saying, 'We'll let you know!' instead of shrugging. So then of course everyone thought there was going to be another one. Kids started asking the teachers about it and eventually the three of us were hauled into Ms Lovell's office.

'You really don't quit, do you?' she asked, but she was smiling. She let us sit on the squashy sofa she kept in her office for special visitors and sat herself on one of the tiny chairs the Year Ones used. 'I've had a lot of questions from pupils and staff,' she said, leaning forward, hands clasped under her chin, 'asking me when our Pride protest is going to be.'

We looked at one another guiltily. 'We never said there'd be one at school,' I said.

'I know,' she nodded. 'But I think it might be a good idea.'

I sat up, blinking in surprise.

Ms Lovell sighed. 'I owe you all a bit of an apology. Especially you, Jamie. I thought your posters were just attention-seeking, and that this whole thing would blow over in a few weeks. I didn't stop to consider that it's something that affects your whole life. I should have listened better. So, I'm sorry.'

I hoped someone was filming this in secret. How often did head teachers apologise to kids? This might be a world first.

'Just because I don't understand something doesn't mean I should dismiss it as unimportant,' Ms Lovell went on. 'You're never too old to learn and I should know that.' She looked at me. 'I'm sorry for not doing more for you.'

I nodded. I didn't want to say, 'That's OK', because it wasn't really.

Daisy noticed the awkwardness and swooped in. 'So, you want to do a school Pride?'

'I do,' Ms Lovell said. 'I think it would be a wonderful opportunity for everyone to learn and to celebrate. And to protest, of course,' she added quickly.

I nodded again. 'I like it. We could have a big assembly explaining the history behind Pride.'

'And a picnic on the field and everyone could come dressed up?' Daisy suggested.

'Yeah,' I grinned. 'And we could tell Stevie what

we're doing and they could put it on social media.'

'We can't put children online without adult permission,' Ms Lovell cautioned us quickly. 'But a small write-up of the event might be nice. Speaking of which, did I see the three of you on the cover of the local paper?' Her eyes twinkled.

I felt myself going red. 'Yeah, that was us.' There was a moment of silence and I twisted my fingers around in my lap. 'Ms Lovell . . . do you think either of the secondary schools will listen and make the changes we want?'

She thought for a moment. 'If you'd asked me a few weeks ago, I would have said no,' she said eventually. 'But now . . . Who knows? The world suddenly feels full of possibilities, don't you think?'

I wasn't sure. Maybe I'd never be entirely sure of anything. But that didn't mean we shouldn't keep trying.

Ms Lovell clapped her hands together. 'That's decided

then. School Pride for everyone. Parents could come too, after school – we can have a proper garden party. We can fundraise for a charity . . . Would you like to help the school council to choose one, Jamie?'

And just like that, School Pride was happening.

*

Over the next week, the school went Totally Rainbow. Bunting of all colours was strung across the assembly hall, the little kids in Year One and Two painted rainbows to stick in the windows, and there was a delivery of an enormous box of Pride flags of every sort of stripe imaginable. I didn't know what half of them meant, so we had a great PSHE lesson finding out which flag represented which identity, before they were strung up and hung from the ceiling.

I saw the flags twice a day, during assembly and lunch, and every time my heart expanded so much it was difficult to breathe. I kept waiting for someone to say they didn't like them, or that they had a problem with them, but if anyone complained I never heard about it. For once, everyone in the school felt united. I hoped that if there were LGBTQ kids who weren't Out yet, they'd remember what this was like, and how much everyone around them supported them.

The parents had been invited for the after-school picnic on the playing field, and my mum and dad sent their slip back straight away, promising to be there. Ash's mum also said she'd be going, but Daisy's mum apparently wouldn't say either way. That didn't surprise me – Denise was still angry about the police station stuff.

The afternoon before the official day of School Pride, Ash and I stayed behind to help unbox some of the crisps and snacks that had been delivered for the picnic. We worked efficiently to undo all the cardboard boxes and made sure everything got a price sticker. We'd decided to donate the profits to a charity that helped transgender kids, and I was hoping we'd raise enough to be able to order one of those huge novelty cheques that are the size of a door.

'I'm sorry about before,' Ash said suddenly.

I looked at him. 'About what?'

'About asking you to pick me to go to secondary school with.' He sniffed, nostrils waggling. 'I shouldn't have said anything. It's not my choice.'

'It's not, but you can always tell me how you feel,' I said. 'You don't need to say sorry, Ash.'

'Maybe not, but I want to.' He stepped on one of the empty cardboard boxes to crush it. 'Because even if we don't go to the same school, we'll still be best friends, won't we?'

'Of course we will!' I almost dropped the crisp packets I was holding. 'Ash, you'll be my best friend right until the end of the universe. Daisy as well,' I added.

He smiled, a real smile, his eyes crinkling in the

corners. 'We'll get together after school and the holidays.'

'Always,' I said, smiling back. 'Promise.'

And the last bit of tension I'd been holding in my chest melted away. We'd be alright, all three of us would, whatever happened.

*

School Pride was incredible. It was a fairly quiet day during the school day itself (though we did have a rainbow-themed lunch with the mashed potatoes dyed blue and everything), but after school things really took off.

The school always does garden party fundraisers once a term, so everyone is used to staying behind to play the tombola or buy some fizzy pop and crisps, but this was different. Everyone got changed into rainbow clothes (me, Ash and Daisy were all in yellow, white, purple and black), painted their faces and stuck ribbons in their hair. Miss Palanska tied a pink-and-cream striped flag around herself like a sash, and Ms Lovell put on a t-shirt she'd had made that said 'I ♥ MY LGBTQ STUDENTS', which was amazing!

All of us spilled outside carrying tables and chairs and set them up on the playground. There was a sweets stall, a second-hand book stall, a chocolate fountain, balloon modelling, and even sour-faced Mr Hill had joined in to run the White Elephant table, his only concession to the dress code a rainbow badge on his lapel. We had a disco going under the wooden gazebo by the field, and a local storytelling drag queen called Mama G was doing a dramatic telling of *Where the Wild Things Are*, to the delight of some of the smaller kids.

The parents and other adults started to arrive around half three. Me and Daisy went to stand by the gates to stamp their hands with a rainbow stamp and take their invitations off them. It was amazing to see so many adults wearing rainbows and glitter, and – this part made my heart leap – coming with their partners who were the same gender as they were. I hadn't realised just how many queer adults sent kids to our school, but it was becoming obvious that our school was a riot of rainbow flags, which had just been hidden away most of the time.

My parents – dressed in yellow and purple and black – looked nervous when they first arrived, but soon broke into big smiles as they saw the party in full swing. Olly came as well. I'd half been expecting him to turn up in one of his skin-tight dresses and big wigs, but he'd kept it on the down-low for once, wearing jeans and a t-shirt, but with sky-scraper high heels and a feather boa.

'Party of the *decade*,' he declared, ruffling my hair before waltzing over to the White Elephant. 'Hello there, Mr Hill,' I heard him drawl. 'Remember me?'

Daisy covered her mouth as she laughed. 'He's brilliant.'

'He's a pain in the bum,' I said. 'But yeah. He's OK.'

I fanned through the invitations in my collecting box, trying to figure how many there were. 'How many do you think we've let in? It feels like hundreds.'

'Maybe more,' Daisy said, trying to count the slips she held too. 'This is more than Ms Lovell usually gets for her events, I'm sure of it.'

I tried to count in fives but ended up dropping some of the slips. 'Heck.'

'Jamie?'

'I'm alright, just let me pick these up.'

'Jamie!'

'What?'

'Look.'

I raised my head.

Waiting patiently in front of us was Mr Dean, the head of St Joseph's Academy for Boys. Behind him were about a dozen students in the St Joseph's uniform. They all, even Mr Dean, looked very nervous.

I stood up, clutching the slips of paper hard, and stared at them. What did they want?

Mr Dean stepped forward, and cleared his throat. 'We were wondering,' he said, 'if we could come and join in your School Pride?'

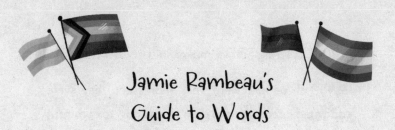

Jamie Rambeau's Guide to Words

PRIDE

Pride, when you're talking about the parade, is a celebration and a protest for people who are lesbian, gay, bisexual, transgender, or otherwise queer. It's a chance to celebrate your own and other people's identity and also to protest ongoing discrimination and the struggles felt by members of the LGBTQ community.

Lots of cities have Pride Parades or celebrations for everyone to join in with and lots of families go together!

The suggestion to call the movement 'Pride' came from L. Craig Schoonmaker, an American activist. Though the first 'pride march' took place the year after the Stonewall riots in New York, the first Pride march in London took place in 1972, and the annual event was officially renamed 'Lesbian, Gay, Bisexual and Transgender Pride' in 1996.

In 2015, L. Craig Schoonmaker said about Pride:

'A lot of people were very repressed, they were conflicted internally, and didn't know how to come out and be proud. That's how the movement was most useful, because they thought: "Maybe I should be proud."'

18

My mouth dried up like the Sahara, and my legs seemed to have turned into lead. They wanted . . . to join . . . in? But this was *our* school, our School Pride. This was mine.

Mr Dean gave a small, embarrassed smile. He nodded back at one of the boys. 'Keyan's little sister comes here and she told him about today,' he explained. 'We've never done an event like this at St Joseph's, and I thought we should come and see how it's done. The boys wanted to come too.'

Daisy's face had frozen into a sort of pained look. Her mouth was twitching as if she was trying not to let some words escape.

I felt much the same as she looked. I wanted to scoop up the whole of our School Pride party in a big sack and run away with it to safety, so no one else could get to it, and it could be ours, safe forever. But then . . .

I glanced at the boys behind Mr Dean. Two of them were wearing tiny enamel pin badges with rainbows on them. Another was looking at the party with the most wistful look on his face that I'd ever seen. I suddenly felt like dirt.

'You can come in,' I said, stepping to the side. 'Just tell Ms Lovell you're here, OK, because you haven't handed in a slip.'

The boys beamed and grinned, and rushed towards the playground, disco and stalls, whilst Mr Dean walked past me, giving me another small smile. I watched as he headed over to Ms Lovell.

'What did you do that for?' Daisy hissed when the visitors were out of earshot. 'He won't even let you go to his school without making you pretend to be something you're not. And you've let him into *your* party!'

'It's not *my* party,' I said. 'It's for everyone. If the boys at St Joseph's have never had a Pride party at their own school, then they're welcome to come here. Mr Dean might not want me at his school, but I'm not going to keep people out just because he has.'

Daisy's eyes went wide and a bit shiny. 'You want to give him a chance?'

'I'm not going to be as bad as him,' I said. I put my box of slips under my arm and turned to look at the party. Mama G the drag queen was doing *We're Going on a Bear Hunt* now, and Olly was joining in. Mr Hill was counting out change and the disco was blaring that old song *Time Warp*. The boys from St Joseph's were scattered here and there – one was having his face painted, some of them at the disco, two of them buying some sweets from Miss Palanska, who was running the stall with her girlfriend.

Pride was for everyone. That's what I wanted it to be, no matter who showed up and how mean they might have been to me. It wasn't up to me to be a gatekeeper and tell people they couldn't join in. That would have just made me as bad as they were.

Daisy took my hand. 'I think that's everyone,' she said, nodding at the empty driveway. 'Shall we go and join in?

*

The party went on way past the advertised time, finishing with Olly and Mama G doing a duet of *Killer Queen* in the gazebo, using the megaphone as a mic between them. The boys from St Joseph's had reluctantly gone home with Mr Dean an hour before, with rainbow faces and enough sugar in their systems to floor a rhinoceros. My parents were watching Olly with amused looks on their faces. Fluff from his moulting feather boa was floating through the air and settling in people's hair.

Ash was tidying the stalls, as he liked to do at the end of these sorts of things, and me and Daisy were helping. Well, we were helping a bit. It was best to let Ash do things exactly as he wanted or else he got annoyed that we'd done it wrong.

'A success, I think,' Daisy said, sweeping with a dustpan and brush. 'We should do it every year.'

'We won't be here next year,' I pointed out. 'Maybe we can gate-crash the next one, though, like the St Joseph's lads did.'

'I still can't believe you let them in,' she said, dusting her pan off into a bin bag. 'I would have told them to get lost.'

'They might not ever get a Pride at their school, though,' Ash said from where he was stacking boxes. 'It isn't their fault their head teacher is an idiot.'

'True.' Daisy put her brush down. 'I was thinking of getting back at them. But that's not how we should be thinking, is it?'

'We don't want to be as bad as them,' I said. 'I don't, anyway.'

'Jamie?' I looked over. It was Ms Lovell and she was holding her phone. 'The local paper would like a photo of you, if that's alright?'

'Non-stop publicity around here,' I sighed, then grinned. 'I'm coming.'

I left Daisy and Ash and followed Ms Lovell over to the rainbow-bunting-draped gazebo, where Mama G, my brother, and a lot of rainbow flags were waiting for me.

'I saw you let Mr Dean and his students in,' Ms Lovell

said as we crossed the playground. 'That was very mature of you.'

'Thank you.'

'I hope seeing what a positive place we created here will inspire Mr Dean to rethink his intake policy,' she said.

I shrugged. 'Even if it doesn't, we helped people feel happy and safe for a few hours.'

She smiled at me. 'I'm going to miss you next year, Jamie Rainbow.'

I laughed. 'My mum hates that, by the way.'

'Well, you're not your mum. What do you think of it?'

I picked up a non-binary flag off a table to hold for the photo. 'I don't hate it. Maybe it could be my stage name when I'm a super-famous actor. But deep down . . . I'm Jamie Rambeau, and I always have been. I don't want to be a gimmick.'

She nodded. 'How wise. You're yourself, aren't you?'

'Always,' I said. Then I climbed up onto the gazebo to smile for the camera, proudly holding up my flag amongst a kaleidoscope of colours and love.

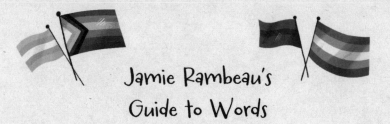

Jamie Rambeau's Guide to Words

Androgyny

Some people think you have to look **androgynous** – that means looking a bit like a boy and a bit like a girl at the same time – to be non-binary, but that isn't the case.

You could have a massive lumberjack beard or wear a dress like Jessica Rabbit and still be non-binary. It's not dependent on what you look like.

You can't guess someone's gender just by looking at them!

19

We didn't change the world. Not right away at least. But we did change a few things, in the end.

I was trying to pay attention to Miss Palanska's Maths lesson when Ms Lovell poked her head around the door.

'I'm sorry to disturb you all,' she said, 'but can I borrow Jamie for a little bit?'

'As long as you promise to return them.' Palanska winked.

Happy to be getting out of Maths, I grabbed my bag and escaped into the corridor with Ms Lovell. 'Am I in trouble?' I asked. Best to know where you stand straight away when you've been pulled out of class.

'No. Why, have you done something wrong?' Ms Lovell asked, making a comedic face of suspicion. Then she grinned. 'I think you'll like this, actually.'

We crossed the hall and went down the corridor to her office. The door was wide open, which made me feel less nervous. But then I spotted, of all people, Mr Dean from St Joseph's Academy for Boys, standing with his hands behind his back like he'd been handcuffed. For a wild moment I thought he'd been kidnapped by Ms Lovell.

'Jamie,' he said pleasantly as I went in. 'Nice to see you again.'

'Hi,' I said, not returning the sentiment.

'Take a seat, both of you,' Ms Lovell said, leaving the door open and pushing her own chair on wheels around the desk. 'Jamie, Mr Dean called me the day after our School Pride. Said how grateful he was that you'd allowed his students to join in.'

'We're going to copycat and do a Pride of our own, just before the summer holidays,' he said. I noticed he sounded a bit nervous, nothing like the man who'd tried to ignore me at the parents' meeting – which felt like a lifetime ago. 'If you don't mind?'

I shrugged. 'Pride doesn't belong to me.' What did he want – my permission?

Ms Lovell cleared her throat. 'That's not all we talked about, Jamie.'

I looked at Mr Dean. A tiny spark of hope started to kindle in my chest but I tried to ignore it.

He didn't exactly smile, but his expression was kind. 'When we first met, Jamie, I have to admit that I thought you were . . . a bit of an attention-seeker.'

I frowned.

'I've since learned that's not true. From what I've heard from your teachers, you've been the exact opposite of attention-seeking until recently. It's . . . people like me who've forced your hand, if you like.'

I nodded, feeling unsure. Where was this going?

'I saw your protest,' he went on, 'on the top of the Council House. I couldn't believe that any kid would do something like that. So reckless, and yet so . . . brave. The paper approached me for a quote and all I could think of was the amount of trouble you'd be getting into. I found out you'd been let out without charge – it was only then that I could actually sit and think about what you'd done, and why.'

I glanced at Ms Lovell. She was smiling.

Mr Dean leaned forward slightly. 'I'm an old man, Jamie,' he said, wryly. 'I was brought up to follow rules and keep doing so even if they weren't fair. You've made me see that sometimes, to be heard, to get your point across, you have to break the rules.' He picked a brown A4 envelope up off the table, and held it out for me. 'It might take another year to organise,' he said, 'but I'm putting forward this proposal to our Governors this Friday.'

Feeling bewildered, I took the envelope and opened it. A heavy bunch of papers, stapled together on one side, slid onto my lap. I picked them up and turned them over to see the title page. As I stared at it, the blood in my head suddenly rushed through my ears, like the roar of an express train, as my thoughts travelled full speed from worry to delight.

'Like I said,' Mr Dean said quickly at the sight of my reddening face, 'it likely won't happen for September, and there are other things to think about logistically, but—' He stopped as Ms Lovell held a hand up, her eyes on me.

'Are you alright, Jamie?' she asked.

I nodded, still staring at the page.

PROPOSAL TO CHANGE SCHOOL NAME TO:

ST JOSEPH'S ACADEMY FOR YOUNG PEOPLE

SUBMITTED BY MR ANDREW DEAN, M.A.

'For young people,' I whispered in a sort of croak.

Mr Dean nodded. 'That's right. What do you think?'

I swallowed. The decision I'd put off for so long was right there in front of me again, like a fruit ready for picking. But it felt different now. After everything that had happened, all the heartbreaks and worries, and then all the celebrations and joy, it felt almost too sudden. I was on the verge of getting what I'd asked for, and it scared me. I knew there'd still be consequences for picking St Joseph's, not all of them good. Daisy might be upset, and maybe Ash would be worried I thought he couldn't cope by himself. But neither of them were ever going to stop being my best friends.

Choosing now wasn't about choosing a side. It was about choosing hope, for the future. Even if Mr Dean's proposal fell through, the fact that he'd tried meant that his school was the place for me. 'I think . . . do you still have any places for September?'

He sagged a little in relief. 'You know there's changing rooms and toilets and things to sort out yet, but I promise we'll do our best to—'

'I know,' I said. 'You've just shown me that you will. So, can I? Come to you in September?'

He grinned. 'Jamie, we would love to have you.'

20

Six months later

I straightened my tie in the mirror, and checked my badges were twisted round the right way. Mum always insisted we have a photo for the first day of school, and she'd even managed to get Olly to look what she called 'Presentable' for the first day of his last year of college. He was applying to theatre school for next year, and was incredibly stressed about it. For once, I was the totally chill one.

'Ready,' I said, thundering down the stairs and

standing beside my brother, who had deferred to peachy-pink lipstick and clear nail polish for the event.

'Calm down,' he chided me, as Mum opened the camera on her phone. 'You're like a human whirlwind.'

'I'm excited,' I explained. 'Aren't you?'

'Heck no. The sooner I'm out of that place the better. I need to be somewhere that recognises my genius.'

'Smile!' Mum said, vaguely threateningly. We did so, and she took ten photos in rapid succession. 'Thank you, you're dismissed,' she said.

We relaxed, and went to find our bags. Mine was a Ms Marvel one this year, with the superhero colours streaming out of a lightning-shaped flash in the middle. I'd got a keyring dangling from the zip with a photo of me, Ash and Daisy in it, all grinning and waving candy floss from the Summer Fair in the city. There'd been no rooftop shenanigans that time, though we did get stuck at the top of the Ferris wheel for twenty minutes after a technical fault.

I stared at the photo for a moment. The fact I'd be walking to school without Daisy for the first time in seven years pulled at my insides in a persistent ache. We'd made plans to meet at the skate park after school though. That made me feel a bit better.

I shoved my bag on to my back and had another look at myself. My blazer was a bit too big, and my tie was a bit too long, and my trousers had those horrible gathers at the back so you can grow into them. I looked like any other kid on their first day at secondary school. Scared and small.

I gave myself a smile.

Mr Dean's proposal had been accepted by the governors – this would be the last year that St Joseph's was an 'Academy for Boys'. There was a huge list of things to sort out, from the toilets to the changing rooms to the uniform (skirts and dresses were on it now, alongside trousers, to the bewilderment of some of the older students). All suggested changes would be put to the students first, in case they could think of any ways to make things even better.

It was more than I'd dared to even hope for during the most worrying part of last year. The memory of fretting about schools, and how I'd be seen, and whether things would ever get better sometimes still crept up on me and made me feel guilty and sad. But then I'd remember everything we'd accomplished, me and Daisy and Ash and everyone else. The rooftop protest. The School Pride. The school visit from a non-binary author, and another from Mama G. There had been a celebration party thrown by Stevie and the University Pride Society after Mr Dean's proposal was made public. We'd raised loads of money for a transgender kids' charity as well.

Things weren't perfect. I still had to weigh up the risks

of choosing one public toilet over another and I still had to sigh loudly when strangers misgendered me. I was being a lot louder about that sort of thing now, which sometimes made Mum and Dad tense. But they were trying. We hadn't changed the world. But we'd made a start. We'd made a difference.

With everyone's help, we could carry on doing just that.

There was a knock at the door, and I was jolted out of my daydream.

'It's Ash!' I yelled. 'I'm going!'

'Bye, sweetheart.' Mum flew into the room and kissed me on the head. 'Have a wonderful day. Find out about that drama club, won't you?'

'I will. Don't forget I'm not coming straight home.'

'Text me when you're on your way back, then.' She stood back. 'Have a good day, Jamie.'

I smiled. 'Bye.' Then I reached out, and opened

the door to the next bit of my life. Jamie Rainbow no longer, but the same person I'd always been.

Proud.

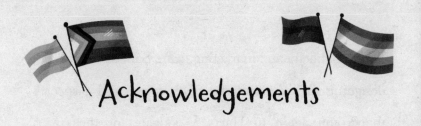

Acknowledgements

Jamie would not have been written without the inspiration and efforts of those who came before. Alice Oseman, Rhea Ewing, Ben Pechey, Harry Woodgate and ND Stevenson, thank you for your words, your art, and your stories. You helped Jamie find the courage to be themselves.

Infinite thanks and love must go to my wonderful agent, Claire Wilson, who encouraged me to finish the story I was afraid to tell (and wasn't really supposed to be writing at all). Thank you for believing in my left-field ideas.

Thank you to everyone in my fantastic team at Hachette, including my marvellous editor Lena McCauley who has been *Jamie*'s champion from the start, Dominic Kingston and Beth McWilliams for being the dream publicity and marketing team, Samuel Perrett for designing such a wonderful book cover, and a special thank you again to Harry Woodgate for the cover illustration, which I will never ever get tired of looking at – Harry, I owe you my life.

Thank you to Lizzie Huxley-Jones, Marieke Nijkamp and L. R. Lam for the early encouragement. And to Alice Oseman, Sophie Anderson, Emma Carroll, Nicole Jarvis, Non Pratt, Alex T. Smith and Louie Stowell for the later cheerleading! Thanks to Alice and Darran for dealing with my emotional garbage at least twice a week, to Olly and Sana for lending me your names, and to Mama G for making a guest appearance!

And thank you to my family, for everything. I love you.

Resources

Childline

A free, private and confidential service to help anone under 19 in the UK with any issue they're going through.

Childline.org.uk

Gendered Intelligence

A trans-led and trans-involving service that runs youth groups, a support line, and carries information about health services.

Genderedintelligence.co.uk

Mermaids

Supports transgender and non-binary children until their 20th birthday, with a help line, training, and web chat.

Mermaids.org.uk

Switchboard

A safe space for anyone to discuss anything, including sexuality, gender identity and emotional wellbeing. Phone operators are all LQBTQ.

Switchboard.lgbt

The Mix

has information and support for anyone between the age of 13–25. Connect with experts and peers who provide support and tools for everything from homelessness to finding a job, from money to mental health, from break-ups to drugs.

themix.org.uk

AT THE
STRANGEWORLDS
· TRAVEL AGENCY ·

**EACH SUITCASE TRANSPORTS YOU TO
A DIFFERENT WORLD. ALL YOU HAVE
TO DO IS STEP INSIDE . . .**

About the Author

L. D. Lapinski lives just outside Sherwood Forest with their family, a lot of books, and a cat called Hector. They are the author of *The Strangeworlds Travel Agency* series, and the standalone *Jamie*.

When they aren't writing, L. D. can be found cosplaying, drinking a lot of cherry cola, and taking care of a forest of succulent plants. L. D. first wrote a book aged seven; it was made of lined paper and Sellotape, and it was about a frog who owned an aeroplane. When L. D. grows up, they want to be a free-range guinea pig farmer.

You can find them on social media @ldlapinski or at ldlapinski.com